Ruth Anne,

May you live, laugh, and love... with passion!

Mary Jane Smith

At Last

An Ageless Romance

Mary Jane Smith

Bloomington, IN

Milton Keynes, UK

AuthorHouse™
1663 Liberty Drive, Suite 200
Bloomington, IN 47403
www.authorhouse.com
Phone: 1-800-839-8640

AuthorHouse™ UK Ltd.
500 Avebury Boulevard
Central Milton Keynes, MK9 2BE
www.authorhouse.co.uk
Phone: 08001974150

First published by AuthorHouse 6/28/2006

ISBN: 1-4259-1847-6 (e)
ISBN: 1-4259-1846-8 (sc)

Author's photograph by Al Gamertsfelder

Library of Congress Control Number: 2006901972

Printed in the United States of America
Bloomington, Indiana

This book is printed on acid-free paper.

WordShack Publishing proudly brings you the work of a new talented author, Mary Jane Smith. WordShack began life as a web publisher in early 2002 and quickly gained critical worldwide acclaim for our award winning website, and the literary quality of work displayed from previously unpublished authors.

The authors displayed on wordshack.com are now enjoyed and reviewed by thousands of readers and authors in 140 countries around the world.

Our mission is exemplified in our corporate statement: "The author's first step to greatness." We search out the best new storytellers from around the globe and provide an opportunity for you to read their work in print.

This book represents our most recent foray into the world of traditional book publishing. After you have enjoyed ***At Last,*** please visit us at www.wordshack.com for information on our other high quality books.

WordShack Publishing is a privately owned trans-Atlantic corporation with offices in both the United States of America and the United Kingdom. Readers wishing to contact us may do so at: useditor@wordshack.com or ukeditor@wordshack.com.

Lynda Blankenship, CEO – North American Operations
Ben Bernstein, CEO – European Operations

Acknowledgments and Dedication

Heartfelt thanks go to all those who encouraged, supported, and aided this endeavor, especially Marilyn Daniels, Raymond Smith, and Richard Otani, Jr.

This book is dedicated to Laura Gennett Smith, my mother and model of the indomitable spirit of woman, whose confidence in my ability has made all the difference.

Preface

Since the beginning of time, women have been slaves to their hearts. It all started with Eve, who, tempted to explore the Garden of Eden on her own, left Adam to fend for himself. Then, remembering that he had willingly spared one of his ribs for her, her heart won out and she returned to stay by his side, for better or worse. Thus began woman's eternal quest for love.

Even in this twenty-first century, women are often torn between following their heads or their hearts. Admittedly, it's a rare occasion when the two lead to the same place. Times have changed. Women's roles have changed; however, little has changed in the hearts of women. No matter how forward-thinking, evolved, or feminist she may be, today's smart, edgy fashionista is still letting her heart lead her around by the nose (plastic though it may be).

Every generation is presented with new issues that challenge and test. Now, in the age of a longer life expectancy, fifty is the new thirty. Women who have spent the earlier part of their lives making others' needs their priority are now ready to grab some happiness for themselves. They're just not sure where to look for it. Today's woman faces a shortage of available (and desirable) men. And the older woman has the slimmest of the pickings. If you aren't convinced, just join a singles' club, and check out the ratio of women to men. Eight or ten to one is the norm. Supply and demand have a way of forcing us to adjust, if not reinvent, our social mores to accommodate our needs. In other words, we look elsewhere, find another way, and push the boundaries of acceptability.

For the first time in the history of our society, it is no longer unusual for a woman to be involved with a younger man. Nearly one-third of women in their forties and fifties have relationships with younger men. Not so long ago, eyebrows would have raised and tongues would have wagged at the sight of an older woman escorted by a man her junior. Gossips would have had a field day calling the attraction a fortune-hunting scheme on the part of the young man or a sexual romp with a boy toy on the part of the woman, reminiscent of the predatory Mrs. Robinson in *The Graduate*. Finally, society is beginning to view the older woman/younger man relationship as an acceptable option.

Another reason for the breaking of this last taboo is that baby boomers have raised their children much differently than their parents raised them. Mothers have taught their sons how to cook, do laundry, and generally be softer than their firm, Depression-aged grandfathers, and more self-sufficient than their often-spoiled fathers. They've encouraged their daughters to be stronger and more financially independent. Therefore, their daughters might be less sensitive, perhaps even less feminine. Consequently, some younger men find women their age too aggressive and overbearing for their taste. They prefer the attention of a woman who has already made her mark rather than playing second fiddle to a younger woman's ambition.

In *At Last,* Olivia Townsend finds herself facing many of the issues plaguing women today. Her happily-ever-after dreams have been squelched – she's divorced and alone and afraid of being hurt again. She's locked into a career she has no passion for, and dreads each day employed in a job she hates. She realizes her prospects for a relationship are slim to none, and accepts it as the lesser of two evils – better to be lonely alone than lonely in an alliance with the wrong man. No wonder she's skeptical when an attractive younger man takes more than a passing interest in her. Although she has trouble trusting his motives, the heart will have what the heart will have, and she succumbs to her own heart's desire for love.

In the end, can she follow her head or does she, like Eve and so many of her daughters, become a welcome slave to her heart?

Prologue

. . . and his eyes blazed, searing my skin through to the depths of my soul. Hands, strong and relentless, took control, igniting every nerve as they expertly traced the path to my pent-up heat.

A shiver trickled down my spine as I remembered those hands, their smooth, bronzed surface, and slow, masterful movements. I rolled away from my journal onto my back, the old mattress squeaking in protest. Air fluttered against my skin as I watched the ceiling fan above me paddle an easy breeze through the room. This room had become my sanctuary since the breakup. From all sides, it reflected me. Posters of the Beatles and Monet's *Water Lilies* hung side by side. Jane Austen's novels shared a shelf with J.D. Salinger's *Catcher in the Rye.* An orange traffic cone, stolen for me by my first love, sat on the floor next to a desk with drawers jammed full of cards holding flowers pressed and dried as a remembrance of important events all but forgotten.

How could I have let it happen *again?* Once, well, it happens. But twice removes any doubt that I'm a fool. True, Rick was the most exciting man I'd ever met. And when it came to looks, he was off the chart. But I wasn't born yesterday, so how could I have been so blind, so naïve, so. . . gullible?

It's not as if I hadn't questioned his motives, because I had. I had questioned them from the very beginning. What is blatantly obvious now had been easily explained away. Perhaps I had blinded myself to the truth because, had I known, I would have missed the most glorious time of my life. I would never have drifted on a wave of desire that crashed through the barriers I had built, leaving me floating helplessly in a sea of love, to be tossed and pulled, dipped and dragged at will.

He had pursued me relentlessly, carefully courting me, plying me with attention, skipping not one detail of the planned seduction. And it had been perfectly calculated, and perfectly executed.

Chapter One

He leaned back comfortably in the huge leather chair, hands crossed over his generous girth. He knew he held all the cards and was obviously enjoying the grip he had on my future. "So tell me why, Ms. Townsend, out of all the candidates for this position, I should choose you."

Not because my heart's in it, I thought, but I needed this job, since a corporate reorganization was claiming my current position. So I had better come up with something to say, and fast. "The reason you should choose me is simple. I can get the job done accurately and efficiently. My experience and skills are a perfect fit for your needs. For example . . . "

I hate this. It's a no win situation. I hate knowing that even if I succeed, I will have lost. Interviewing for a job is nerve wracking enough, having to feign total confidence and omniscience while being drilled on your past, present, and future. That's what they want, someone with godlike qualities. No matter that the job is merely a mid-level accounting position, the successful candidate must be experienced, but not rigid; assertive, but not overbearing; objective, but never indifferent; knowledgeable far beyond the job description, but never beyond her supervisor's competence. And if, after this torturous process concludes, I am the Chosen One, the Victor, I will have landed a respectable position with a reputable company that others will envy, a position that will very gradually and systematically sap the life right out of me.

Okay, I admit it. My name is Olivia Townsend and I'm a hopeless romantic. I can't help it. It's not a choice, as I see it, just a natural tendency that can't and shouldn't be stifled. Even at a very young age, my head was in the clouds, daydreaming of faraway places where all was beautiful and life was one blissful experience after another. In school, I preferred reading and writing to arithmetic. And the sciences were never of interest to me. I've always enjoyed anything where imagination comes into play, where there are no facts or figures to adhere to. I have always loved the beautiful, whether it be art, music, dance, or literature.

It is the bane of my existence that I have no talent in the arts. The only sign of any cultural aptitude turned up in high school when I first discovered I had a flair for writing. I always aced my writing assignments with minimal effort. And I loved all my college English classes.

However, in an attempt to be practical, I had majored in accounting. Since I was a shrinking violet in those days, quiet and shy, never wanting to be the center of attention, I figured that accounting would be a perfect fit for my personality and, of course, practical. Sales, marketing, and public relations were out of the question. And, like it or not, I had always excelled in math. Bottom line was I needed to be able to make a living after graduation. I couldn't afford to pursue any pie-in-the-sky career in the arts that I loved. So here I am applying once again for a job I already hate.

I stopped the car at the end of the drive and reached into the mailbox for the day's mail. For a week now, I'd been waiting for a rejection letter from Leonard Kistler and Company. I'd been unable to interpret the reactions of the interviewer as genuinely interested or just polite. I figured if I couldn't tell, it must have been bad. But there was no letter from them today.

I pulled into the drive, and as I emerged from the car Angie came running out of the house. "They called! They called!" she yelled, excitement flushing her cheeks. At forty-nine, my sister was still a beautiful woman. She resembled our mother with her smooth olive skin and thick black hair cut short, framing her face in luscious waves.

Her body had more curves now than when she was younger, the fuller figure adding to her Latin look.

No one ever took us for sisters. I'm taller, longer of limb and shorter on curves. Shoulder-length auburn curls that refuse to be tamed bounce about my head, taking on a life of their own. My eyes are the only evidence of my Italian heritage. By far my best feature, they're huge and round, almost too large for my face, and dark as ripe olives, my mother used to say. She always teased that she chose the name Olivia for that reason. Luckily, I don't look my age at thirty-eight. Good genes and a good moisturizer go a long way to conceal at least six of those years. And I definitely don't feel my age. In fact, I find it hard to believe that I'm closing in on forty.

Breathless, Angie reached the car, "They want to schedule another interview," she gasped.

It was my first day at my new job, and I was so nervous and trying so hard to remember who was who. Navigating through each department during the orientation tour, I was introduced to almost everyone in the building. Finally alone in my new office, I breathed a sign of relief and started to dig into the vast pile of information I'd been given to absorb.

Bent in concentration, I didn't even feel his presence as he leisurely leaned against the doorframe, a confident smile on his lips. His deep, rich, baritone "hello" startled me so that I jumped, sending the round container of pens and pencils over the edge of the desk and onto the floor, scattering everywhere. With lithe swiftness, he smoothly swooped down and retrieved all that had fallen, positioning it exactly as it had been, and then gazed into my eyes in a way that, just for a second, made me forget to breathe.

"Sorry. Didn't mean to startle you," he said in that velvety voice.

"Oh no, not at all," I lied, struggling for composure. I stood up behind the desk, feeling like a total klutz.

"Welcome to Leonard Kistler. I'm Rick Sloane. I'm in sales, foreign sales," and he held out his hand, still smiling.

I leaned over the desk to shake hands, taking in his suave manner and exotic good looks. He was tall, dark, and handsome, but not typically so. He had an All-American look, but with an Asian twist. Dark eyes and golden skin gave him an air of mystery. What secrets lie beneath that fascinating surface, I pondered, my imagination running wild? Solid and muscular, Rick handled himself with ease and grace. I could see why he was in sales. Aside from his obvious good looks, that combination of winning smile, innate composure, and sultry voice clearly enabled him to, as they say, sell refrigerators to Eskimos, and surely had charmed many a woman out of her panties. Where did that come from, I wondered? He was, after all, just introducing himself.

"Olivia Townsend, accountant," I floundered, and shook his hand. Could I sound like any more of a nerd?

"Well, Olivia Townsend, accountant, my pleasure. Good luck on the job. I'm sure we'll meet again," he said, and disappeared down the hall.

After our brief encounter, I saw nothing of Rick in the weeks that followed. I was submerged in the task of creating balance sheets and income statements that accurately represented the financial status of the company.

Every morning, as I drove the sleepy streets of Laurel, Ohio to work, I reminded myself how much we needed the money, how Angie had sacrificed everything so that I could get a degree, and how I couldn't let her down. It became my mantra. And then, for another ass-aching day, I would surrender myself to spreadsheets and flowcharts.

The sales department was on the second floor, accounting on the fourth, so I was not likely to see Rick, but ever since our first meeting, I secretly looked forward to our paths crossing. One afternoon, as I headed out to grab a quick lunch, I decided to take the stairs. The exercise would help clear my head of facts and figures.

Gaining speed down the stairwell, I rounded the second floor landing just as the door opened, and ran straight into Rick, sandwiching him between the door and my body. Without skipping a beat, he grinned down at me and whispered, "Miss me?"

Stunned for a moment, I stood there, our bodies touching, not really wanting to move away. Suddenly embarrassed by our close proximity, I staggered back a step, trying to regain some semblance of dignity. Too late.

"Seriously, are you all right?" he inquired in a gentlemanly fashion.

"Fine. I'm just so sorry," I fumbled.

"Seems like I am always surprising you."

"Yes, I guess so."

"Let me make it up to you. How about lunch? It's the least I can do."

"Really, it's not necessary. Anyway, it was my fault."

He ignored my last comment and asked, "Where would you like to go? How about Bobbie's Bistro? They always have a good selection," and without further discussion, he escorted me down the steps and a block down the street to the restaurant.

Seated in a booth toward the back of the little bistro, I found myself peering over the top of my menu at this interesting man. He was impeccably dressed in a dark suit, white shirt, and power tie. He wore no jewelry except a Cartier watch. He was all about quality. That was obvious. I decided he was a cross between Bruce Lee and Cary Grant, taut and firm, suave and debonair.

He caught me staring at him over the menu. "See anything you like?" he asked, a devilish smile creeping over his face.

I sank behind the menu and cleared my throat. "I can't decide," I said ambivalently, thinking two can play this game.

Why didn't I wear the navy Ann Klein suit today, I scolded myself silently? It was a classic style, understated and flattering to any figure. My weight had been a touchy subject ever since my parents' accident. It was then that I started using food as a source of comfort, and consequently became a very chubby child. During my freshman year of high school, I took control of my eating habits and slimmed down, but I've always had to fight the tendency to medicate with food.

Instead of the trim navy suit, I had chosen a pale yellow sheath with matching jacket. I had fallen in love with it when I saw it hanging in the boutique window, never taking into consideration that it was linen. So now I found myself a mass of wrinkles sitting across from Mr. Smooth.

After we ordered, Rick, the filet of sole, and I, a Cobb salad, we fell into easy rapport. He told me that he was born in Hawaii, his mother a Japanese American. They had moved to Ohio when he was a baby because of his father's work as an engineer. I vaguely remembered adult conversations about the new "mixed" family in town, and my parents' adamant live-and-let-live convictions. Rick was the oldest of six children, five boys and a girl. "They were determined to have a daughter," he laughed.

He had been studying to be a doctor, attending medical school at Ohio State University, until his family needed financial help to put his brothers through college. He had dropped out of med. school to take a job in sales. He shocked me when he said that he was twenty-nine. He seemed older, more mature. Nine year age difference, I calculated quickly. I felt slightly relieved. We could be friends without the office gossiping of romance.

Little by little, as we ate and talked, I opened up to Rick about my childhood, my parents' accident, and Angie. Rarely did I ever discuss my family with anyone, but I didn't mind telling him; in fact, I found myself spilling out every detail.

"Charles, come on! They're waiting!" my mother called up the steps to my father. This was not uncommon. My mother moved at lightning speed at all times. She was always into something - cleaning, cooking, fixing. Even during dinner she was up more than she was down. No grass grew under her feet. She spent a lot of time waiting for Dad.

To my mother's constant irritation, my father had only two speeds, slow and slower. He moved calmly, quietly, and deliberately. But when he did something, it was done right.

After twenty-three years of marriage, neither of them had adjusted to or accepted this difference in their personalities. It was still a point of contention between them, but it was just about the only one. They had what others, including me, dreamed of - a happy, loving relationship.

"Charles, pleeeease! We're behind schedule already!"

"Well, you don't want to be down the road and wonder if you remembered to turn off the iron and close the windows, do you?"

"I already checked those things, and besides, the girls will be here. Now you'll be okay, won't you girls?"

"Sure Mom. We'll be fine," I assured her.

"I know you will. Livie, your sister's in charge, and Aunt Rosa will be checking on you several times a day. Angie, if you have trouble of any kind, call Aunt Rosa right away, or if it's an emergency, call the police."

"Mom, I'll take good care of Livie," Angie promised as she smiled at me and tousled my hair. "Now you should get going."

I was excited. I was going to be spending time alone with my older sister who I worshiped. Angela would be twenty-one next month and I was ten. She knew all the secrets about boys and makeup and clothes, and I couldn't wait for us to have some real quality girl talk. "Don't worry, Mom, we'll be fine. Just forget about us and have a good time."

"I could never forget about my girls! Now give me some hugs," which we gladly did at least three times each.

"All right, I think we're ready." Dad always got uncomfortable when the good-byes lasted too long. "You two behave yourselves. You have the numbers where we can be reached, and we'll call you tomorrow," Dad said, giving us each a big hug and kiss.

Angie and I followed our parents out to the driveway and stood waving and blowing kisses until they were completely out of sight. It was the last time we ever saw them.

Three days later, they were touring Canada, en route to the shrine of Sainte Anne de Beaupré in Quebec, when an oncoming car careened over the center line of the two-lane road slamming directly into my parents' car. There was no time to swerve out of the way. We were told that they were dead on contact. The driver of the approaching car, a young woman, had been trying to commit suicide. She did not succeed.

A month later, on her twenty-first birthday, Angie became my legal guardian. It was a lot to take on, but she would have it no other way. She dropped out of college, never finishing her senior year, got a job at J.C.Penney's and took care of me. I attached myself to her like an extra appendage after the accident, but she never complained. I can't imagine how she didn't resent me. She gave up a degree, hopes of a career in clothing design, and her independence because of me.

Our extended family of aunts, uncles, and cousins were always available for us, but Angie and I learned to depend and rely on each other almost exclusively. She became my whole world, my closest friend and confidant, my rock.

What would I do if I didn't have my big sister to turn to? After the accident, I blamed myself in some skewed way for my parents' death, and felt unworthy and undeserving of happiness or anything good in my life. Of course, I was too young at the time to understand or acknowledge these feelings, or the fact that I feared being alone more than anything in the world. So it was not surprising that I became obsessed with the thought of losing Angie. I was only ten, but I knew from experience how quickly loved ones could be snatched from you.

Rick listened quietly, and when I had finished, he reached for my hand and squeezed it with compassion. "I'm so sorry about your parents. That had to be rough, especially at that tender age."

"It was, but my sister was there for me, and held us together. I owe her everything." I blushed, suddenly feeling that I had revealed too much.

"She's obviously an amazing person, but I bet having you there helped her cope with the loss as well."

"I hope so, but I think I was more of a burden than anything else."

"I can't imagine anyone considering you a burden," he said with an open and cool directness, and I felt a tiny quiver of pleasure.

"But you had to give up med. school and your dream of becoming a doctor for the sake of your brothers' education. That was no small sacrifice."

"You do what you have to do. I never thought of it as a choice or a sacrifice. I just did what was necessary for the family." He lifted his water glass in a toast. "To family," he said with a sheepish grin.

Clinking my glass against his, I repeated, "To family," and couldn't help thinking that I could really like this guy.

Lying in bed that night, my thoughts wandered to Rick and our conversation. He had been so open and easy to talk to. He obviously had a sense of humor and enjoyed a challenging repartee, but there was also a softer, more sensitive side to him that I found very appealing. And his commitment to his family had impressed me.

His looks, though unconventional, were striking. I pictured his dark brown eyes crinkling with laughter, the high cheekbones, and full sensuous lips. The low-pitched melodious voice vibrated in my mind, the very thought of it curling my toes. Too bad he's out of my league, I thought. Too young, too handsome.

Suddenly it struck me that this was the first time since my divorce from Roy that I had reacted to a man in that way. Determined never again to risk the devastating rejection and heartbreak of a failed marriage, I had carefully protected myself from any romantic involvement, drawing the line at friendship. It may not have been nearly as exciting, but it was infinitely safer. No need to worry though, because why would someone as obviously appealing as Rick show an interest in me?

Chapter Two

After our lunch together, Rick made it a point to stop by my office every now and then, and I looked forward to his visits. We talked about our mutual love of the theater and art, and his passion for classical music and golf. He was truly a Renaissance man.

By my one-year anniversary on the job, we had become good friends. He was the light of my days at work and his friendship helped me through the monotony of debits and credits. Things were going well, but I sensed that Rick, to my surprise, wanted more. I was flattered by his interest, but our friendship was too important to me to risk it for romantic involvement. And besides, we made the original odd couple seem like a perfect match. He was head-turning gorgeous and I was, well, sort of attractive. He was of Asian ancestry; I was Italian, with a pinch of German and English. And the age difference alone made it out of the question. If we tried and failed, which was most likely, it would cost us everything. It would be too awkward to go back. No, I couldn't take the chance. I wouldn't.

One Friday, Rick dropped by my office, and after some small talk, invited me to go golfing with him on Saturday. "It'll be fun," he encouraged.

"But I play like a girl. I won't be able to keep up, and you'll be bored."

"With you, never! You worry too much. You'll be fine. And by the way, I don't need to be reminded that you're a girl" he grinned with sparkling eyes.

"Okay, but you've been warned!"

Saturday morning was sunny and clear. The grass was wet with dew, and the air still crisp from the cool night. Rick picked me up at seven, and after introducing him to Angie, we whizzed off with our clubs stuffed in the back of his bright red Mustang convertible. I was feeling young and free and happy, the best I'd felt since Roy and I had split. And then he ruined it all. As we pulled up to a stop light, he turned to me and said, in a far too serious tone, "Olivia, I want you to understand that this is a date, our first real date."

He caught me completely off-guard. He knew that I would never have agreed to go if he had asked me for a date, but what could I do now - ruin the day with an argument, or go along with him and straighten things out later. I opted for the latter. I was in too good a mood to take on some heavy discussion, so I answered him, as casually as possible, "Oh, if you say so."

He flashed me that irresistible smile and said, "I do."

Golfing turned out to be a blast. Riding a golf cart with Rick at the wheel was more fun than most amusement rides as he drove wildly over hills and dales to swoop down and retrieve balls without slowing down in the least. He had such agility and grace. He kept me laughing, allowing no time for me to feel self-conscious about my swing, our age difference, or the fact that we were on a so-called date.

After golfing, we had a casual lunch at the Leaping Lizard, and then stopped by a small art gallery. The gallery was filled with paintings in oils, acrylics, and watercolors, as well as other art mediums including sculptures, stained glass, and pottery. We browsed, admiring various pieces.

I was inspecting several colorful pottery bowls shelved in a corner of the room, when Rick took my arm and turned me to face him. His expression darkened, becoming almost austere, and in his deep, chocolate voice he said, "I don't want you to worry. I won't be kissing you," and with that, he picked up the beautifully enameled bowl I had been considering, took it to the cashier, and bought it for me.

That's how we started dating. After numerous attempts, I gave up trying to reason with him. He was a salesman, after all, and a born negotiator. It was futile to try to beat him at his own game. And I had to admit I enjoyed being with him. He had set the parameters of our relationship, and had observed them at all times. I was glad because it allowed me to enjoy our friendship to the fullest without worry of it escalating into something physical.

Relieved as I was, my romantic tendencies led me to wondering if he had any desire to kiss me or if he too was relieved to be off the hook. What was I thinking? He had obviously promised not to kiss me to spare himself and me from any misunderstandings about his intentions. It was his way of making it clear that he agreed things were best left as is and nothing more would come of it. I chalked the whole dating thing up to satisfying his male ego, proving that he could date me if he chose to.

The rest of the summer flew by. At least twice a week, Rick and I got together, attending a concert or ballet, going to the theater, golfing, or if it rained, playing backgammon and picnicking on the living room floor in front of the television. Rick kept track of our dates, and usually, when he arrived, he would announce, "This is date such and such," and I would merely laugh.

One Sunday afternoon in early September, Angie left for the annual neighborhood street party, toting two large rectangular foil pans filled with rigatoni, and said she'd be staying late to help with the clean up. Rick and I were going to the tennis courts. I finished dressing in white T-shirt and shorts, pulling my hair back into a ponytail. Rick picked me up and, in his usual way, declared it to be Date Nineteen. He looked very appealing in his white polo shirt and navy shorts. We played several invigorating sets of tennis, then picked up a pizza, and ate it at our favorite place, the living room floor.

Rick had been on the wrestling team in high school, and after we finished eating, he began demonstrating several wrestling holds using me as his opponent. Before I realized it, I was pinned down and he was over me.

"Don't move," he murmured softly.

I was frozen in place and couldn't move if I tried, but I didn't try. My heart pounded in my ears. My mind raced. This is it, I thought. Why hadn't I backed off before it came to this? This was the beginning of the end of our friendship. Why must he push the envelope now, when everything was going so well? But what could I do? Might as well get it over with, I decided.

Rick lowered his face to mine, and ever so gently his lips touched my skin, slowly and tenderly outlining my mouth with tiny kisses. "Don't move," he repeated.

But it was too much to ask. Against my will, my lips moved, seeking his. I never expected it to be this way. I was floating and flying, completely under his spell. And as we explored deeper, I felt my every nerve stand at attention. Under my closed eyelids I swear I saw red sparks stream across the darkness.

I had no idea how long we had been completely absorbed in each other when the grandfather clock in the foyer struck the hour. Rick backed off and pulled me to my feet. Struggling to gain my equilibrium, I tried to remove all evidence of what had just happened, adjusting my hair and wiping my eyes of smeared mascara.

"Well," Rick said in a long exaggerated whisper.

"Well yourself," I said, not knowing where to look exactly, too embarrassed to look him in the eye. We had only kissed. Not once had he laid a hand on me. Yet we had crossed the boundaries of friendship. Now what? The inevitable, I thought. I get involved and my heart gets broken. Why couldn't we have left things the way they were? We were having so much fun. Our friendship was surely doomed now.

The following week I avoided Rick, begging off when he suggested we see a movie. I knew it was childish, but I didn't know how to proceed since the kissing episode. After a week of internal dialog and turmoil, I came to the conclusion that, since the relationship was already set in motion, I had to play it out, for better or worse, or never see Rick again, ending our friendship anyway. And I knew I wasn't ready to sacrifice the entire relationship for safety's sake.

Once I made peace with the idea, Rick and I fell back into our old, comfortable habits, adding the new dimension of romance. My only request was that we take things slowly. By now, Rick had an innate sense of how I was feeling almost before I could put it into words. He could read me like a book. He paid attention to everything I said and did. I realized that no one had ever taken the time to understand me the way he did. It felt good, very good.

Christmas approached with the usual festivities and frustrations that accompany the season. Meanwhile, things were heating up with Rick and me. We had shopped for a tree the week before, and had barely managed to set it up and decorate it between passionate embraces. Angie had stared at the tree with its lopsided star and drooping garland, shrugged her shoulders, and walked away muttering that it was "not exactly the traditional look," as we fell to the floor snorting with laughter.

Rick and I agreed to spend Christmas Eve together. He was spending Christmas Day with his family. Many of his brothers lived out of town and were coming home for the holiday, and he wanted to spend as much time with them as possible. He invited me to join them, but I wouldn't think of leaving Angie alone on Christmas Day. She and I were having Christmas dinner with Aunt Rosa, Uncle Louie, and our cousins, and, although she wouldn't actually be alone, I had to be with her.

It had been difficult selecting a gift for Rick. A tie was too boring. Besides, I had to admit he had better taste in ties than I did. A shirt, sweater, or clothing in general seemed rather thoughtless. A book was too impersonal. On my umpteenth shopping spree to the mall, scanning the display window of Ball Jewelers, I spotted a two-tone gold and silver ID bracelet. It was masculine, classy, and personal. That's it, I decided. I had his first name engraved on the top, and my initials on the back. I was giddy with anticipation now that I had his gift.

Cooking is not my forte, but, against my better judgement, I offered to fix dinner for Rick on Christmas Eve. Angie was having dinner with the Langleys next door. I was on my own. Various types of fish - smelts, squid, cod - and pasta with oil and anchovies comprised our traditional Italian Christmas Eve meal, but it was an acquired taste, to be sure. I thought it best not to subject Rick to such ethnic flavors on my first cooking attempt. The menu would be simple and uncomplicated - broiled halibut marinated in lemon, rice pilaf, asparagus spears, salad, and rolls. Angie's Christmas cookies would serve as dessert.

All was going well. Everything was ready, except the halibut. I would wait until Rick arrived to place it under the broiler, since he usually ran late. At seven, the doorbell rang. To my surprise, he was on time. I poured him a glass of his favorite Cabernet Sauvignon, and warned him not to enter the kitchen under any circumstances. It made me nervous to have anyone watch me cook. I slid the halibut under the broiler and began spooning the rice and asparagus into serving dishes. The broiler started smoking. Within seconds, the smoke alarm went off. Rick stood in the doorway, anxious to see what was causing the smoke. I pulled the fish out of the oven, as he peeked around the corner. "Everything okay in here?" he yelled over the alarm, knowing he was in forbidden territory.

"Yes, yes, just a little smoke." I tried to act unconcerned. The halibut would be blackened and not Cajun style. Apparently, I had placed the fish too close to the broiler.

"Anything I can do?" he ventured.

"Yes, grab a pillow from the sofa and fan that damned smoke alarm in the hall, would you please?" I snapped, losing control.

Rick disappeared, and in seconds the alarm stopped its shrill blare.

After trying to calm my frayed nerves and convince myself that everything was fine, I headed for the living room to announce that what was left of dinner was served. I had expected to find Rick under the smoke alarm, fanning it with the pillow, since the rooms were still heavy with smoke. Instead, he was relaxing in one of the tapestry-covered wingback chairs near the fireplace.

"Trying to make me earn my dinner tonight, are you?" he teased, as he read my mind and handed me the battery he had removed from the alarm. In the midst of my culinary crisis, that simple solution had never occurred to me.

"Hope you're in the mood for smoked halibut," I said, regaining my composure, and we laughed our way into the dining room.

Dinner was a success despite the charred halibut, thanks to Rick, who could smooth over any situation. Afterward, we carried our coffees to the living room where we sat on the sofa, admiring our handiwork on the strange-looking tree.

"It's got a unique, whimsical quality," Rick said, trying his best to put a positive spin on our shoddy work.

"Delightfully unstructured," I agreed, "but definitely a Martha Stewart reject."

I retrieved Rick's gift from under the frumpy tree. "Merry Christmas," I said, as I kissed him and handed him the small, square box.

He got right to the business of ripping off the Christmas wrap. When he saw the jeweler's name on the box, his eyebrows raised in question and I could see he was a little uneasy. He didn't normally wear jewelry, other than a watch. My heart sank. What was I thinking buying him jewelry? Suddenly, it was all I could do to keep from snatching the box from his hands and throwing it out the window. I had wanted it to be so special, and now I was sure he was going to hate it. I cringed as he lifted the lid off the box and silently removed the bracelet. He read the inscription, then fastened the bracelet onto his wrist, holding his arm out for inspection. In one smooth movement, Rick pulled me close to him and held me in his arms. "Thank you, Livie. It's perfect," he whispered in my ear. "I'll wear it always," and he kissed me softly on the mouth.

I was still basking in the joy that Rick was pleased with the bracelet when, a few minutes later, he reached into his pocket and pulled out a tiny box, obviously a ring box, and placed it in my hand. A dozen scenarios flashed through my mind. A friendship ring. An emerald, my birthstone. An engagement ring. Oh my God, an engagement ring? What would I do?

"Aren't you going to open it?"

A very long minute had passed while I contemplated the possibilities. I held my breath and opened the box. It was a rectangular amethyst stone with triangular diamonds on either side set in a gold mounting. "Oh, Rick," I exclaimed, "it's exquisite." My worries had been senseless.

He slid the ring on my finger. "It's only a preview of what's to come."

His comment left me fearful, yet excited about the future.

Huge snowflakes were falling as we left the house and walked hand in hand down the street. Christmas lights, some solid white, others in holiday colors, reflected on the snow, creating a glow in the midst of the dark night. We said little as we took in the beauty of the season together. *Silent Night*, it felt so right.

Our relationship was no longer that of just friends. Even I had to admit that I was in love. Rick had booked a room at Hunting Valley Lodge for New Year's Eve. It was a package deal that included dinner and dancing, champagne at midnight, and a buffet breakfast the following morning.

"Angie, what should I do?" I moaned. Angie was the best counselor, psychologist, and advisor you could ask for. I turned to her when I was confused or in doubt of which way to go. And it was always just common sense - *just* common sense that I, the emotional one, couldn't figure out for myself. I invariably came away with a fresh perspective after talking things out with her.

"How do you feel about Rick, really?" she asked, her eyes narrowing in on me.

"I'm happy when I'm with him. We always have a good time together. I guess that's what bothers me, other than the fear of being hurt. Is it too good to be true? Does he want me for me, or is there something else?"

"You mean an ulterior motive?"

"Exactly."

"Has he given you any reason to believe he has some hidden agenda?"

"No, not really, but he's so good-looking, and young. Nine years and three months younger than I, but who's counting. He could have any of the other girls at work, probably any woman he wanted. So why me?"

"Well, there are no guarantees in life. Or love. I think you're underestimating yourself and your own worth. Liv, you're a beautiful, intelligent, and caring woman. Any man would be lucky to have you in his corner. I like Rick and I can see how you light up when he's around. This decision is one that only you can make. Just be sure you don't let fear or feelings of inadequacy influence you."

As usual, talking to Angie made it clear to me what I had to do. I had to see this thing through. I had to go for it, put myself out there again, frightening as that was.

As I was packing my overnight bag, I caught my reflection in the full-length mirror attached to the closet door. For what I realized was the first time in quite a long while, I looked at myself and saw not a soon-to-be middle-aged has-been, but a desirable, even sexy, woman. Granted, there were areas that could use some air brushing, and others that were no longer as perky as they had once been, but as I let the chenille robe fall to the floor, I ran my hand along womanly breasts, a trim waist, and soft, slender hips. Not long ago, I would only have seen the flaws. I had to admit that seeing a younger man had been a boost to my chronically sagging ego. Rick made me feel alive and invigorated. He had single-handedly brought me back to life and out of the state of dormancy that I had inhabited since my divorce. I now viewed myself as I was reflected in his eyes – as an attractive, sensual, and very desirable woman.

The lodge was an hour and a half away, nestled in a valley of rolling hills. The sun was setting behind the farthest snowy ridge when we arrived. Our room overlooked the lake, which was coated with a silver sheen of ice. Rick carried our two small bags to the room, and then left to check when dinner was to be served, allowing me time to dress for the evening. It was not black tie, so I had brought my street length little black dress. It was plain, flaring at the bottom to fall into soft folds at my knees. Sparkling chandelier earrings and my new amethyst ring were the finishing touches. When Rick returned, he stood back for a moment and whistled. "Wow, I won't be able to take my eyes off you tonight!"

"That's the idea," I said in the sexiest voice I could muster.

In ten minutes, Rick was dressed and we were being led to our table. The room was arranged with round tables for eight, each covered in white linen with red poinsettia centerpieces. We were seated with three other couples. After everyone exchanged greetings and introductions,

Rick whispered to me, "I didn't know we'd be sharing a table. This was not exactly what I had in mind."

"It'll be fine," I soothed.

Couples around us devoured the standard fare of prime rib, baked potato, green beans, and salad, while Rick and I barely touched our food. We had other things on our minds.

When the musicians took their places, we knew we were in trouble. The youngest of the trio had to be in his sixties. They began with "New York, New York" and it went downhill from there. When they began strains of the "Beer Barrel Polka," we just looked at each other and laughed. We managed one dance as the band did their rendition of "Fly Me to the Moon." Rick held me so close I felt the stare of a hundred senior eyes upon us, but I didn't care.

It was only ten o'clock when Rick announced to me, "We're out of here." I couldn't have agreed more. We caught the knowing looks of the others at our table as we wished all a Happy New Year and fled.

Rick drew open the drapes to let the moon light the room with silver beams and shadows. He opened a bottle of champagne that had been chilling in the ice bucket. We toasted the wonderful year we had together, and the hope of even better things to come.

Rick removed his jacket and tie, and gently guided me to the bed. Our lips met, parting to let in the hot warmth of each other while he smoothly unzipped my dress. When he unhooked my bra with one hand, I gasped at his expertise. Then his clothes fell to the floor and in an instant he was over me, his mouth again on mine, seeking and giving new pleasure. He was everywhere, stroking and tasting, as I soared higher and higher, moaning at his touch. At a leisurely pace, but with single-minded thoroughness, he worked his torturously exquisite magic, igniting a heat inside me that rose and boiled, demanding more and more. The sweet anguish of arousal radiated down my spine and through every nerve. I'd never before known the level of desire and urgency that had my body screaming for fulfillment. I cried out his name as I arched against him, and united, we moved as one until finally we writhed with pleasure and quivered in total joy and satisfaction.

He had brought out the woman in me as no man ever had.

Chapter Three

January launched the busiest time of year in the Accounting Department. Closing out the year's transactions, and preparing financial statements and audit schedules kept my nose to the grind for the next three months. Rick was traveling a great deal of the time, introducing several new product lines to the European market. We saw each other in between his travels and my long hours.

Work finally let up a little in April. Rick had a business trip to France scheduled for the end of the month. "Come with me," he urged. "I'll finish my work in a couple of days, and I'll have the rest of the time to show you Paris, the south of France, and maybe even Monte Carlo."

I hadn't taken any time off since I had started with Leonard Kistler the year before. I had accrued plenty of vacation time, and after the crunch of the last few months, I knew I could use a break. I couldn't think of anything better than to be in Paris with Rick.

The first day of our journey, however, I was convinced I'd made a huge mistake. A shuttle bus picked us up at the Laurel airport at five in the morning and deposited us at Cleveland International at seven-thirty after many interim stops along the way. We could have driven to Cleveland in an hour, but I had argued that when we returned, it would be easier to let someone else do the driving back to Laurel, since we would probably be exhausted. Rick had reluctantly acquiesced, but he was not happy as we jostled along in the shuttle. I would not argue the case in the future.

Our itinerary was Cleveland to New York to Paris since all direct flights were booked by the time I gave Rick my final answer. Once in

Cleveland, we had to check our luggage, get through security, and find our gate in time to board our flight to New York at eight-fifteen. It was a close call, and if Rick had not known his way around the airport, we would never have made it. We arrived at Kennedy International a little over an hour later. Again, we hustled to be at the gate in time for boarding. And then we waited.

We were informed that our flight to Paris was delayed because of a minor technical problem. That was not news I wanted to hear. Bad enough having to wait after rushing all morning to get there, but as far as I was concerned there were no *minor* technical problems when it came to flying. I was a nervous flyer at best. Knowing there was a problem with the plane didn't help matters. Rick tried to keep me occupied with card games and magazines during the layover. Finally, we heard the announcement that boarding would begin at twelve-fifteen. We took off shortly after one, as I sat, white-knuckled, praying for a safe flight.

In my mind, I had pictured flying over Paris, sighting the Eiffel Tower, the Arc de Triumph, and Notre Dame Cathedral. I had to stop romanticizing everything. Instead, we arrived after three in the morning Paris time in the dark of night. I was dead tired from the day's travels and my only interest was in getting to our hotel and flopping into bed. I hadn't slept a wink during the flight. Rick, however, had snoozed soundly for at least six hours. Was this a preview of things to come on our romantic getaway?

We arrived in our room at the Hotel du Quai-Voltaire with its tall windows overlooking the Seine, its period furniture, and a bidet. How totally Parisian, I thought. In minutes, I was snuggled under the duvet with Rick, the day's frustrations vaporizing. Everything could wait. It was my first night in Paris with the man I loved. "Thank you for bringing me to Paris," I sighed.

"You've heard the saying, 'When in Rome, do as the Romans do'?" he asked, with a Cheshire cat grin spread across his handsome face.

"Yes, of course," I answered, wondering where this was going.

"Well, I'm told the French say, 'When in Paris, do as the Parisians do.'"

"Oh, is that so? And what *do* the Parisians do?"

"Make love, naturally."

"Well, then, who are we to defy tradition?" I laughed, and soon any remnants of the misery of the day melted away and the only thing that mattered was the heat of our love. Rick gave me a night to remember on my first night in the City of Light.

I had expected to be on my own my first day in Paris. Rick would be working, calling on clients all day, but, to my surprise, he had arranged a tour guide for me. Madame Gerard, the wife of one of his contacts, was meeting us for breakfast at Les Deux Magots, a café at six place St-Germain-des-Pres, once a legendary gathering place for French intellectuals. When Rick had asked his business associate the best way for me to see the sights, Monsieur Gerard had insisted that his wife would gladly show me Paris. "No one should see Paris for the first time alone," he had declared.

I was a little nervous as we arrived at the café. I wore a casual cotton dress in sage with tiny pink rosebuds and matching sweater that I had bought for the trip. But now, I wasn't so sure that it was the right choice. Everywhere I looked, Parisian women were fashionable and very sophisticated.

Madame Gerard was seated at a table when we arrived. Rick escorted me to the table and greeted her warmly. "Olivia, may I present Madame Gerard. Madame, I'd like you to meet Olivia Townsend."

"How do you do, my dear? Please, sit down. I have ordered cafés au lait and croissants for us." She was, I guessed, in her sixties. In her dark pantsuit with a red scarf at the neck and her hair sleek in a chignon, she was the epitome of Parisian chic.

"Madame, thank you for taking the time to give me a tour of your beautiful city," I stammered.

"Please, call me Solange. And it is always a pleasure to see Paris through the eyes of one viewing it for the first time."

Rick finished his croissant, gulped down his coffee, and, with a kiss on the cheek, was gone.

"Olivia, this is your day. Where would you like to begin?" Solange asked.

"There's so much to see, but I don't think I'll believe I'm really in Paris until I see the Eiffel Tower. Pretty touristy, I guess," I said, apologetically.

"Nonsense, the Eiffel Tower is the symbol of Paris. The Tour Eiffel it shall be."

From that moment on, we hit it off like old friends. From the Eiffel Tower, Solange took me to the Louvre where we spent hours admiring the masterpieces of art. I was amazed at how the *Mona Lisa's* eyes seemed to follow me wherever I stood. "It was not only a matter of art for Da Vinci, but also mathematics and geometry," Solange explained.

After the Louvre, we stopped at a sidewalk café for a glass of Beaujolais, a fruity wine from Burgundy, and lunch, which consisted of quiche and salad. I had always wondered how the French could be noted for some of the best and richest foods, and yet, in general, be quite trim. I learned from Solange that the French eat well, but lightly. And they walked a lot of it off, I was finding out, as Solange suggested we stroll along the Champs-Elysees to the Arc de Triumph.

The sun shone brightly, tinting the already glorious architecture a golden hue. We crossed the Seine to the Ile de la Cite and Notre Dame. Entering the cathedral, the cool musty air of the great stone structure welcomed us into this hallowed house of God. The sun lit the stained glass windows, beaming shafts of rose-colored light from above, inspiring and humbling all those who visited.

It had been an enchanting day, one that I would never forget. I thanked Solange profusely when we said goodbye in front of the Hotel du Quai-Voltaire, hugging and kissing her on each cheek. It made me feel very French.

I was exhausted, as she must have been, but while I appeared worn and weary, she managed to look as fresh as in the morning.

Back in the room, I napped until Rick returned at six. "How was your day?" he asked.

"*Fantastique*!" I answered in my new French accent. "Solange was wonderful," and I proceeded to recount everything we saw and did. Rick had made reservations for dinner at Le Grand Vefour at the Palais-Royal for nine o'clock. We had plenty of time to relax in bed before dressing for dinner. I thought I could not possibly be worthy of such happiness as we made love in our hotel room after spending a day discovering some of the most beautiful sights in the world.

Dinner was elegant. I wore my favorite little black dress, the same one I had worn New Year's Eve, with a simple strand of pearls and my amethyst ring. We were seated against the banquette next to one of the tall windows facing the street. Rick selected the Roederer Cristal and after a toast to Paris, we dove into the *foie gras*. I ordered the bouillabaisse and Rick chose filet mignon. The food was perfection, and we ate hungrily, trading samples of our entrees despite a few arched eyebrows. We finished with a lavender creme brulee, which we split. Actually, Rick took two bites and let me, the dessert diva, devour the rest.

After dinner, Rick whisked me off to a little club that Monsieur Gerard had suggested. A jazz band was performing the Etta James classic, "At Last," when we arrived and Rick asked me to dance. He held me close and we moved to the music as one.

"This is so perfect," I sighed, as the lyrics floated over us. Whatever spell he had cast over me, I accepted willingly because at that moment I knew in my heart that I was his. And I felt that Rick was truly and completely mine.

"Then I think we should make this our song," Rick said, kissing my neck.

"Yes, definitely," I agreed, thinking that the song was right, this was heaven.

We left the club much later, and aimlessly walked the streets of Paris, arm in arm, feeling the pulse of the city, stopping in a shop here, a café there. It was after two in the morning when we returned to the hotel.

Rick had rushed to finish his work, and said that after a meeting tomorrow morning he would be done. We decided to spend the next day in Paris and then head for the Riviera. I could have stayed in Paris for weeks and not seen everything, but our time was limited, and I didn't want to miss the Riviera. Besides, I felt sure we would return someday.

Solange had pointed out the best shops in Paris on our tour day, but we hadn't had time to stop. While Rick finished up with business in the morning, I decided to do some shopping. I had picked up gifts for the girls at work and the neighbors in souvenir shops, but I needed to find something special for Angie. On the rue du faubourg St-Honore, in the eighth arrondissement, I bought her a lovely silk Hermes scarf. Then, in a lingerie shop, a sales associate assisted me in finding a lacy white camisole, the kind I knew my sister would never buy. I couldn't resist a black teddy for myself, or was it for Rick? Just the thought of him made me smile.

I spent hours shopping for a suitable gift for him, and finally purchased a gold money clip I thought he would like. He hated carrying a bulky wallet in his pocket. The cost was more than I should have spent, but in Paris, nothing was cheap, and after all, Rick had been adamant about paying for all the expenses of the trip that the company wouldn't cover. That was everything from here on out, since his business ended in Paris. He had only relented when I insisted on paying for my own transportation or not go. I would find a way to repay him for the rest after the trip. The money clip would be merely a token of my appreciation and love.

My next shopping splurge was a cream-colored chiffon dress I spotted on a mannequin in an exclusive boutique. It had a V-neck with gathers of chiffon crossing the bodice diagonally. The waistline was fitted with a thin gold belt and the skirt flared to a tea length. I didn't know where I was going to wear it, but that was irrelevant. I had to have it.

As I often did when shopping, I had lost track of time and was late meeting Rick for lunch on the terrace of the Café de la Paix, place de l'Opera. He anticipated as much, ordering ahead for us. We ate the salads *niciose* leisurely, drinking white wine and settling into anonymity while enjoying the variety of faces in this international mingling spot. We watched the Parisians parade by in their finery. As usual, they were all dressed to the nines.

The Musee d'Orsay, housing the Impressionists, was our next stop. It was no coincidence that the Impressionist movement began in Paris with Monet, Manet, Renoir, and many other artists. It was all about catching the light and reflections off of a subject, and where else to perfect it than the City of Light.

Hours later, after sharing the beauty of what I considered some of the most magnificent paintings ever made, Rick and I lay in bed in the late afternoon, languidly kissing, gliding smoothly into arousal, as the tension inside us slowly built to a throbbing urgency. We savored every sensation until the heat bubbled into an uncontrollable rush and peaked with a force that shook and stunned.

We spent our last night in Paris wandering the streets of Montmartre around the cathedral of Sacre Coeur. A street artist drew our portraits in chalk. On the rue Tholoze we caught a view of the city over Paris rooftops. We passed the famous Moulin Rouge, once frequented by Toulouse-Lautrec, preferring each other's company to the crowded nightclub loud with cancan music and dancers. We had stars in our eyes. Paris had cast its spell on us. It was, after all, the city for lovers.

Early the next morning we checked out of Hotel du Quai-Voltaire and headed south for the Riviera and Saint-Tropez in the Renault Rick had rented. We took our time, taking in the delights of the French countryside along the way, and stopped for breakfast of a baguette with cheese and *deux cafés* in a little café just off the road. We continued south, passing fields of poppies and quaint little villages.

By late afternoon, we had reached Carcassonne, where we stretched our legs climbing the ramparts of this walled city atop a hill. Then we traveled through Avignon to Gordes, with the Luberon Mountains on the horizon, and we stopped to take a stroll on the narrow cobblestone streets, past the ancient church, the *pharmacie*, the *boucherie*, and the *patisserie*, to a café where we dined on omelets and sausages.

The sophistication of Paris was long gone. Here, the people led hardworking simple lives. The chic couture and gourmet cuisine was replaced by work clothes and country-style food. The very simplicity gave it its own charm.

Back on the road, we drove the rest of the way nonstop to Saint-Tropez. The area is a playground for the wealthy, known for its nightlife that draws many a celebrity. We pulled into the moderate Hotel Sube where Rick had reserved us a comfortable room decorated in the Provincial style, with a lovely view of the port. After showering and changing into fresh clothes, we went down to Le Café de Paris located in the same building. Neither of us was very hungry, so we ordered a carafe of the local rosé and munched on plates of cheese, olives, and tomatoes.

Gazing at Rick as he picked his favorite Gruyere cheese from the variety on the plate, I wondered at how lucky I was that he had chosen me. Had he not pursued me with such unwavering fortitude, I would not be here vacationing on the Riviera with the man I loved. It went beyond anything I had ever dared to dream for myself. How did I come to deserve this? I don't, I thought guiltily, I'm quite sure of that.

"What's wrong, Liv?" Rick asked just then, jolting me from my reverie.

"Nothing, nothing at all," I answered with a quick smile, shaking off the self-doubt that had shrouded me.

"You looked distant and sad there for a minute," he continued, scrutinizing my face. "Is something bothering you?"

"No, sweetheart, it's just that sometimes I feel so . . . unworthy of so much happiness."

"Is that all? Well, I hope to make you happy for a long, long time," and with that, he leaned over and kissed me in a way that made me tingle all over. "What do you say we go back to the room?" he whispered sensuously in my ear. When I nodded enthusiastically, Rick caught the waiter's attention with a wave and requested, "Check, *s'il vous plait!*"

We barely made it to our room without pulling each other's clothes off. The chemistry we had was undeniable, the tiniest spark igniting an inferno of desire. Uninhibited, filled with the assurance of love, we followed our urges with wild abandon, each of us taking the greatest pleasure in satisfying the other. In the wee hours of the morning we lay spent, exhausted, a tangle of limp limbs.

My stomach growled, and I reached for my purse on the floor beside the bed, remembering the candy bars it held for just such emergencies. Handing one to Rick, we unwrapped the delicacies one at a time, alternately taking bites of the chocolate until both bars were gone, licking each other's fingers of all melted remains. No chocolate souffle in Paris could have tasted as good, we agreed.

In the morning, we ambled about the Saint-Tropez market in the Place des Lices, browsing the vendors' displays of colorful fresh fruits and vegetables, fish, and cheese. At the Café des Arts, we stopped for coffee and croissants, then returned to the hotel, packed our bags into the back of the little Renault, and set out for Cannes.

Cannes, of the famous film festival, with the beautiful Carlton Hotel on La Croisette overlooking the Mediterranean and its ribbon of sandy beach, is a spot on the Cote d'Azur for the jet set to sun themselves in luxury. The Plage de la Croisette, dotted with blue and yellow umbrellas, provides the guests a place to exhibit their carefully sculpted bodies. I was glad to have the chance to see this famous resort, but it felt too ritzy, not our kind of place, and I asked Rick to drive on to Nice. Our time was running short, only two more days before heading back to Paris and the flight home, and I didn't want to miss Monte Carlo.

We arrived in Nice, a bustling metropolis bordering the Mediterranean, just before dusk. We parked the car and walked hand in hand along the Promenade des Anglais overlooking the sea, not wanting to miss the sun setting beyond the horizon, with trails of brilliant orange and pink coloring the inky blue sky.

We had no hotel reservations, and after a few phone calls, found that we had waited too late to get a room. All the hotels were booked. Rick suggested a small hotel where he had stayed occasionally when he was in a pinch. It was close by, in the Vieille Ville, the Old Town area of Nice, but he warned that it was definitely a no frills establishment. I was eager to find anything at this point.

When we got there, Rick rang the bell, and after a minute or so, the door opened.

"*Mon Cher*, Richard!" the petite old woman smiled with delight, creasing her rouged face with even more wrinkles.

Rick obligingly hugged and kissed Madame Sophie on each cheek, introduced me, and inquired whether she had a room that we might have for the night.

"*Bien sur*! Yes, of course! Come in, come in!" she cried, and we followed her inside and down a long, dark hallway to a room at the end of the hall.

It was an odd room, with a mismatch of old furniture, the walls of the room not quite reaching the high ceiling, and a door the top half of which was frosted glass. A fan hung down in the center of the room, slowly rippling the air around. The bathroom was down the hall. "I warned you it wasn't fancy," Rick reminded me.

"It's fine," I assured him, "a little weird, but fine."

After our long day's travel, we collapsed on the cool white sheets in our strange room, grateful to have a roof over our heads and a bed to sleep in.

The next day, after a good night's rest, we wondered down the maze of narrow streets in Vieille Ville. We bought onion pizzas from one of the vendors for lunch. With much hugging and kissing, we thanked Madame Sophie, promising to return to visit someday. She wagged a crooked finger at Rick, admonishing him in her quick French. "What was that all about?" I asked, as we went back to the Promenade des Anglais for one last view of the Mediterranean from Nice.

"You know, just an old woman's ravings. She said that I had love in my eyes and that if I nurture it, it will grow, and someday, it will nurture me."

"What a lovely thought. Your eyes did look a little strange today," I quipped, sensing Rick's embarrassment.

The faded blue of the morning sky met the deep marine of the water, each wavelet reflecting its own sparkling diamond of sunshine. The infinite array of diamonds shone like a treasure chest, almost too bright for the naked eye. We walked the wide boulevard that fronted the bay with rows of grand cafés, villas, and hotels. Our tired, aching feet found their way back to the car and once on the coastal highway, we headed east for the eleven miles to Monaco.

Chapter Four

Traveling in on the Moyenne Corniche, Rick drove straight to the Palais du Prince, the home of Monaco's royal family, knowing how anxious I was to see the home of Grace Kelly. Monaco's reputation for glamour was sealed in 1956 with the marriage of Prince Rainier III to the actress, who he met while she was in Cannes promoting her movie, *To Catch a Thief.* The Monegasques still mourn her tragic death when she accidentally drove over one of the treacherous cliffs of the tiny monarchy.

The Palais du Prince, situated on "the Rock" high above the Mediterranean, resembled a scene from a fairytale. Or Disneyland. It didn't seem real in the perfect setting atop a cliff, with pinkish walls and red and white striped guard houses that looked as edible as candy canes. We witnessed the changing of the French guard, a tradition dating back to the sixteenth and seventeenth centuries.

As a special surprise, Rick had booked us a room at the cliff top Hotel Hermitage, a first class hotel. The room came complete with large mirrors, elegant fabrics and upholstery, deluxe bathroom, and a sumptuous brass bed. The icing on the cake was our own balcony with wicker armchairs to relax in while enjoying the breathtaking view of Monaco.

"I thought you should see Monaco in style," Rick said as he walked me onto our balcony.

"Oh, Rick, I'll never forget this as long as I live!" I wrapped my arms around him, kissing him deeply, without reserve. How true my words would prove to be.

That was all it took. Rick threw me onto the big brass bed, yanking off my clothes with demanding urgency. He slid onto me and I was lost in a whirl of sensation as we fell into our rhythm of love, at first slow and tormenting, then faster and faster to a feverish pace until I was wound so tight I shook. We peaked together, the force rippling through us in waves of splendor.

Afterwards, we lay exhausted, my head nuzzled in against him, feeling the steady beat of his heart.

"Are you okay?" Rick asked, always concerned for me.

"You're just full of surprises, aren't you?" I gasped, still breathless from our lovemaking.

"Do you mind?" Rick asked, stroking my head as it rose and fell with his chest.

"I'd mind if you didn't surprise me now and then, but I don't think I have to worry about that," I smiled.

"No, you don't. Honestly, Liv, sometimes my reaction to you surprises even me. I've never felt so connected to a woman, mentally and spiritually, as well as physically." It was difficult for Rick to open up about his feelings, as it was for most men, and I appreciated his willingness to talk to me about them.

"Me either, to a man, I mean. What I had with Roy was never this . . . intense." Looking back, it seemed almost superficial in comparison. This must be the real deal, I thought, although even now I had moments of doubt, wondering why such a handsome young stud would prefer me to the younger model types he attracted like bees to honey.

Rick chose Rampoldi's for dinner, a well-known restaurant with French and Italian cuisine. Located at the edge of the Casino Gardens, we could conveniently walk to the Casino after dinner. We had decided to dress up for the last night of our trip. Rick surprised me again when he exited the bathroom in tux and black tie, which he had rented, looking positively debonair, the white shirt contrasting his tanned skin and shining black hair. I had slipped into the cream chiffon dress I bought in Paris, complete with gold belt and strappy gold heels. I was relieved that we wouldn't have to walk too far that night. I wore my hair up, with a half dozen little rhinestone flowers placed strategically to sparkle from every angle.

Rick's eyes widened when he saw me and, kissing me on the cheek, he said, "I'm going to be the envy of every man tonight."

I blushed and smiled, thinking how beautiful he made me feel.

He escorted me out onto our little balcony with the to-die-for view of a golden sunset over the royal blue Mediterranean. Facing me, he took my hands in his and slowly and deliberately brought them to his lips, kissing each one softly. Then, holding my hands close to his chest, his dark eyes piercingly focused on me, he said in the deepest honeyed tone, "I love you, Olivia. I need you. I want you. But most of all, I love you."

"Oh, Rick, I love you so much. I'll love you forever," I answered, and we held each other tight and kissed, Rick masterfully taking ownership of my lips and mouth, and I willingly surrendering to his touch. All was perfect with the world, as far as I was concerned; Rick loved me and I loved him. This was what I had hoped and prayed for since I was a little girl - to have the one I love, love me back.

We took a cab to the restaurant, which had been around since the 1950's. It was a charming mix of old and new, with more Italian influence than French. We both ordered pastas, I, the tortelloni with cream and white truffle sauce, and Rick, the ravioli stuffed with crayfish. The food was so delicious we had to hold back from licking our plates. For dessert, the waiter recommended Crepes Suzette, which originated locally and was named after one of Edward VII's many companions.

After dinner, Rick and I walked to the famous Casino built by architect Charles Garnier. It is situated on a terrace with a superb view of Monaco. High ceilings dripping massive chandeliers decorate this gambling palace, and that is exactly what it looks like, a palace. It was originally built for the entertainment of the aristocracy of Europe. Roulette is played in the opulent Salle Europe. Craps tables and slot machines, considered a bit gauche, can be found in the Salle de Jeux Americains.

Once we had toured the Casino and enjoyed the postcard perfect view from the terrace, Rick ordered us drinks at the elegant Salon Rose bar with its female nudes smoking cigars spread across the ceiling, and guided me to one of the craps tables. He bought some chips, kissed me, he said, for *bon chance*, and placed a rather large bet. He won, and then bet everything again.

I was excited, but nervous at the prospect of him losing it all. "Are you sure you should bet it all?" I asked him. I enjoyed playing quarter slot machines now and then, but this was way too rich for my blood.

"Don't worry. You're bringing me good luck!" he said, which made me all the more uncomfortable. It would be my fault if he lost. It was thousands of dollars. The wild look in his eyes told me he was going to bet it all, regardless of my opinion. The dice rolled and again he won. His face was flushed with excitement as he ordered, "Let it ride."

I couldn't believe that he was risking it all. I covered my eyes as the dice rolled down the table.

"Yes!" Rick gasped as his number came up again. I was so relieved when he collected his chips, his winnings totaling more than ten thousand dollars.

Before I knew it, he led me into the Salle Europe to a roulette table. "Why don't we just take your winnings and go?" I pleaded.

"Not now, Babe," he said, sounding not at all like himself, "I'm on a roll!" and he placed a thousand-dollar chip on nineteen black. "For Date Nineteen and our first kiss," he explained. The little silver ball circled the roulette wheel round and round, slowing and bouncing until it settled, miraculously, on nineteen black.

Rick was in a frenzy now, fevered by his winning streak. Luck, however, is a fickle lady. The next five bets were not so lucky for him. He was losing everything he had won, and then some.

"Let's go back to the hotel and our beautiful room," I begged him, but he refused to listen.

"I know I can win it all back. I'm not leaving here a loser," he said in a cold, firm voice that was totally unfamiliar to me. "All I need is a little more cash and I'll win it all back. Liv, lend me the cash and I'll pay you back plus split the rest of the winnings with you," he persisted.

I closed my eyes and sighed hopelessly. I knew I had no real choice but to give him the money, even though I knew it was irrational and he'd more than likely lose it too. But Rick was beyond reasoning with. I had never seen him like this. He was out of control. I was actually fearful of what he might do if I refused to give him the money. He knew I had brought extra funds in case of an emergency. "How much do you need?" I asked guardedly.

"Ten thousand," he snapped, without hesitation.

"What? Ten thousand dollars?" I repeated incredulously.

"What's the big deal? I paid for your whole trip, didn't I? It's the least you can do," he shot back arrogantly.

He might as well have shot me through the heart with a gun. My face paled and I felt a sharp pain somewhere in my middle that threw me back against the wall behind me. I was bent in half, gasping for air. I couldn't see or hear anything, and knew I was on my way to passing out when a strong sharp odor helped clear my senses. A Casino employee had stepped in, waving what I assumed to be smelling salts under my nose. Rick was holding me up by my shoulders.

When I finally got my equilibrium, I shook myself free of him and dug into my purse until I pulled out ten thousand dollars worth of travelers' checks. At a small table nearby, I signed the checks with a shaking hand. Straightening with pride, I then turned and held the checks out to Rick, my eyes meeting his levelly, my face void of emotion. "Here," I said in a clear bland tone, "take them."

He hesitated, and then started to speak, but I cut him off before any words were spoken.

"That should cover it. I hope it was worth the trouble," I said, in as even a voice as I could manage and flung the money at him.

I turned to the Casino employee, asking him to please see me to a cab immediately. As I was ushered to a waiting cab, from the corner of my eye, I could see Rick still scrambling to retrieve the scattered travelers' checks.

This can't be happening, I repeated to myself, over and over, my hands clutching my crossed arms as I sat rocking back and forth, back and forth in the backseat of the cab headed for the Hotel Hermitage. The sudden turn of events was more than I could comprehend. A mere few hours ago, I was the happiest I had ever been in my life. The joke was on me - to be given a taste of true happiness and then, in an instant, have it jerked away. It was laughable really. How could I have thought myself worthy of such happiness? What a fool I was to have thought, even for a moment, that Rick could love me. It was obvious now that he had brought me along on the trip knowing he would need money for his gambling habit. He had probably done it many times before - meet up with a lonely woman, get close enough to invite her on a dream vacation, and then take her for all she's got when she's far away from home and vulnerable. It all made sense now.

Once in the Hotel Hermitage, I enlisted the services of the concierge. I explained that it was urgent that I get back to the States as soon as possible. After much flapping of arms and French chatter, he arranged a helicopter flight to the Nice Côte d'Azur airport. From the east terminal, I would catch an international flight to New York. In five minutes, I changed into jeans and a T-shirt, jammed everything into my suitcases, and was being driven to the heliport.

Only vaguely aware of the jet engines' humming, I looked out the small window to catch a final glimpse of the sparkling lights of the Riviera. How happy I had been there. How we had made love and professed our love to each other. I should have known, I told myself as tears poured down my face; I should have known he didn't want me just for me. I had to marvel at the irony that just hours after I finally opened my heart and told Rick I loved him, it all became clear.

Chapter Five

"There's no fool like an old fool. The worn cliché describes me to a tee," I muttered between sips of the hot coffee Angie had poured. I'd made it back to the comfort and security of home, and now as Angie sliced and diced, preparing our next meal, I unloaded my heavy heart. As I did, I realized that I had never been comfortable with the nine-year age difference between Rick and me, until Paris that is. There it didn't seem to matter. Love was the universal language, and all combinations of lovers were accepted. Now I felt old and foolish at thirty-nine.

I was too embarrassed to cry in front of Angie. Three days had gone by since I had left Monaco and Rick. I had cried a river of tears. Swollen and bloodshot eyes were the only result. The tears had not helped ease the pain of what had happened. Angie had been understanding and sympathetic, but now she thought it was time I picked up the pieces and got on with my life. She was right, I knew, but how do you move on when the pain is still unbearable?

I relived that last night in Monaco again and again, trying to wrap my brain around the reality of it. When Rick first asked me to go to France with him, I had insisted that I pay my own way, but he had said that it was out of the question. Call it macho pride, he had said, but since he had invited me, he would take care of it. I finally agreed, so long as I paid for my transportation and, of course, any incidentals. I had decided, instead of arguing, that I would get him a gift to repay his generosity when we returned, maybe a new sound system for his beloved classical music or the huge flat screen TV he always admired when we were shopping.

The man I witnessed gambling in the Casino was not the caring, playful, loving man I knew. Rick had changed before my eyes into an insensitive, hostile stranger whose gambling controlled him. It had been an ugly transformation. I was aware of how addictive gambling could be; like everyone else, I'd heard of Gamblers Anonymous and the horror stories of what the addiction could do. It was one thing to know of it and a completely different thing to experience it.

If I were convinced that it was a gambling addiction alone that had caused the problem, it would have been easier to cope with the situation. If I could believe that in the beginning Rick's intentions were good, that he hadn't pursued me just to set me up, that it was the Casino and the gambling fever that had made him act the way he had . . . but I wasn't convinced of that at all. In fact, I believed just the opposite - that Rick had, from day one, pursued me in a very planned and calculated manner with one goal in mind - money. He obviously had a taste for the finer things in life. I remembered telling him about the trust fund from my parents' accident somewhere along the line. Angie and I were not rich by any stretch of the imagination, but the insurance settlement from our parents' accident had allowed us to pay off the house and have a nest egg for an emergency. And we had never touched that savings, both of us feeling strongly about not wanting to live off of money received from our parents' death. I had always questioned the reason for Rick's interest in me. Why me? Now the answer was clear - money.

I was easy prey, ripe for the taking. Divorced, older, sheltered - the perfect target for a smooth operator with an over-the-top charm factor. I had to come to terms with the fact that I had been played. It had taken him a while, but in the end, I had fallen for it. I had fallen in love with him.

I had searched for an ulterior motive with Rick from the very beginning, but he had always been above reproach. We started out as friends, after all, and I had been so cautious, aiming to avoid another painful relationship after Roy. I might as well have thrown caution to the wind from the day we met because it had not protected me from this devastation and heartache.

My greatest challenge, next to getting out of bed each morning, was facing my first day back to work. On the commute in, I practiced smiling in the rear view mirror. The forced grin and glazed eyes wouldn't fool anyone, but they had to be good enough to get me through the day. I was sure Rick would not chance an encounter at work, so I was safe there.

As it turned out, I survived the day thanks to the tons of accumulated work piled high on my desk. I buried myself in it, requesting that my calls be held, and worked straight through lunch.

That night, when I walked into the kitchen, Angie pulled a letter from the stack of mail on the counter and held it out to me. "This came for you today. It's from Rick," she announced warily. I took the letter to my room, fell onto the bed, and tore the little ivory envelope open.

Dearest Olivia,
I'm truly sorry things worked out the way they did.
I hope you have it in your heart to forgive me.
Love,
Rick

The note was accompanied by a check for ten thousand dollars.

Not exactly sonnet material, I thought. That's it? No explanation? No mention of getting together to talk things out? Lame was the word that came to mind. Very lame. Obviously, he had no desire to save the relationship. I stuffed the note into my jewelry box where the gold money clip lay, thinking it will serve as a reminder that what we once had was gone. I tore the check into shreds, carried it down to the kitchen wastebasket, and threw it in with the chicken fat and potato peels Angie had tossed in earlier.

My way of coping with this loss was to completely envelop myself in work and family, weaving myself into a cocoon of shelter and safety from everything and everyone on the outside. The days passed in a blur, one an exact replica of the next.

Rick had kept his distance. The note had been his grand finale. To my knowledge, he never came to the fourth floor again and I made it a point to avoid the sales department. I heard he was spending a lot of time abroad, pitching the new price increases to foreign customers.

I returned to my old love of literature and the written word for refuge, and night became a time to read and then, eventually, to write. I waded through each day anticipating its end when, safe in my room, I could open my journal and write. I poured onto paper my heart, the pain, the feelings bottled up inside me.

Once I started, I couldn't stop, writing frantically night after night, week after week, month after month, until, there it was - a novel - an autobiographical novel. I had thought of my writing only as therapy, a way to deal with the pain. I never expected to produce a book in the process. It had served as a kind of emotional cleansing for me. Finally, I could feel almost okay with life again.

After reading my novel, one of my English professors from college put me in touch with a literary agent out of New York, Rachael Cohen, who read my story and said that, with some editing, she was sure she could get it published. I was ecstatic! I had a chance at being published. It was a dream come true.

One hot and humid afternoon in late August, Rachael called me at the office, "Olivia, Horizon House Publishing has accepted *Journey of Love* for publication. It will be in print and on bookstore shelves for the holidays."

Tears welled in my eyes, "Oh Rachael, thank you, thank you so much for making this possible," I cried.

"No need for thanks. Good material makes my job easy. And there's more. Trey, that is, William Henry Osborne III, the publishing guru at Horizon House, is putting together a contract for three more of your novels. He was interested in the story lines you mentioned for future publications and he likes your style. We won't accept his first offer, but he's a fair man, so I'm sure we'll reach an agreement."

I was stunned beyond words. My mind raced. A contract - did that mean a career? Was Rachael saying that I was a writer, a soon-to-be-published author?

"Olivia, are you still there? Can you hear me?" Rachael yelled into the phone impatiently.

"Yes, oh yes, I'm here," I stammered.

"Trey wants to schedule a meeting for next week. How does Thursday work for you? I told him I'd confirm the time tomorrow. You'll have to arrange a flight to New York for Thursday morning. You should come to my office first, around ten if you can manage it. I'll brief you on what to say and not say during your meeting, then I'll deliver you to Horizon House Publishing, introduce you to Trey, and be on my way. We can meet for dinner at La Caravelle before you catch your flight back to Ohio. How's that sound?"

"Fantastic, except for the restaurant. No French restaurants please," I requested quietly.

"Oh, sure, sure, no problem. Sorry, I forgot. Okay, call me when your flight is booked. Gotta go. Bye."

I was still holding the phone to my ear as it beeped annoyingly to alert me that she had hung up. I hadn't noticed. Nothing this good had ever happened to me. Could it be true? Angie, I had to call Angie and tell her the news.

After I repeated my entire conversation with Rachael to my sister, my excitement gave way to fear. "Do you think this Mr. Osborne will like me? Will he still be interested after he meets me?" My insecurities were surfacing.

"Of course he'll like you. Why wouldn't he? He's already interested in your writing. Now don't go sabotaging this opportunity with your fear of success or that low self-image that hovers over you at times like a black cloud. You are worthy of this, Liv. You deserve it. You've already proven it with your writing. The only thing you need is a new outfit for your trip, so we're going to do some shopping, okay?"

"What would I do without you?" I said, knowing I owed everything to Angie.

The elevator ride to the thirty-second floor was making my already queasy stomach nauseous. When the doors opened, Rachael and I stepped out into the plush lobby of Horizon House Publishing Company. Undoubtedly designed to create an atmosphere of success, stability, and longevity, the walls were lined with ceiling-to-floor mahogany bookshelves filled with books the company had published over the years. Above the mantle of a large fireplace hung a period picture of a woman in a flowing gown, seated on the ground under a tree, reading a book. The hardwood floor was covered with an antique Savonnerie rug. A sofa in rich brown leather faced the fireplace with several large winged chairs upholstered in dark velvet flanking either side. Several large ferns fringed the corners of the room. Indirect lighting enhanced the quiet dignity of the room from shaded sconces along the walls.

Rachael checked in with the receptionist, then we took seats on the leather sofa. I noticed that even she was whispering, with the reverence usually reserved for a house of worship. The grandiose decor only made me feel smaller and less consequential than I already did. New York City had a way of making a person feel minuscule, especially a lone woman from Laurel, Ohio.

Rachael could see that I was overwhelmed. "Relax. Trey is a great guy, very savvy. He likes to get to know his people. I wouldn't leave you alone with him if I thought you couldn't handle it. Just remember what I told you, 'Better to say too little than too much,' got it?" she whispered and patted me on the arm reassuringly.

"Got it," I repeated with hollow determination.

Moments later, the heavy door next to the receptionist's area opened, and a tall, slender man, maybe fifty or so, walked toward us in long strides. "Rachael, how good to see you again," he said cheerily in a cultured English accent. His clear blue eyes, intelligent and alert, sparkled with genuine pleasure as they shook hands.

"Trey, I'd like you to meet Olivia Townsend. Olivia, this is William Osborne."

"It's a pleasure to meet you, Mr. Osborne," I spouted, quickly standing and extending my hand.

He shook my hand firmly, smiling as he said, "The pleasure is all mine, to be sure, Ms. Townsend. Now, if you will accompany me to my office, we can chat more comfortably." Turning to Rachael he said, "I will be in touch," and with that he escorted me to his office and Rachael was gone.

"Please sit down, Ms. Townsend," he said as he held a chair for me. His was a corner office, large and bright, with windows on two sides overlooking the jagged skyline of Manhattan. The stuffy sophistication of the waiting room was nowhere to be found here. Black and chrome dominated the modern furniture. The huge desk and credenza had long, sleek lines. Off to the side, near the windows, a black leather sofa and chairs, accented with chrome, surrounded an oval glass and chrome coffee table. The only touches of color were an arrangement of fresh flowers, mostly chrysanthemums, in bright yellow on the table and a modern painting splashed with vivid reds, yellows, and greens hanging on the far wall. Books were piled everywhere, and what I guessed to be manuscripts waiting to be read were stacked haphazardly around the edge of the desk.

"May I get you something to drink, coffee or perhaps a soda?" he offered.

"No thank you, Mr. Osborne. I'm fine." I was afraid I might choke on the first swallow, nervous as I was.

"Please, call me Trey," he said as he sat across the coffee table from me, his legs casually crossed and an arm stretched along the top of the sofa.

"And I'm Olivia," I countered. In his double-breasted pinstriped suit, he looked rather distinguished. I was grateful that Angie and I had decided on the plum Donna Karan suit with pale pink shell, which I had accessorized only with pearl earrings. I no longer wore the ring Rick had given me.

"Well, Olivia, I've read your novel, *Journey of Love*, and I'm very impressed. You have a comfortable style with good character development. It could use a little sprucing up from our editing department, but that is standard procedure. As you can see all around you, I read many manuscripts, and it's seldom I find one as well written as yours, especially since it is your first."

"Thank you, I'm so glad to hear that," I answered self-consciously, as my peaches and cream complexion turned more peaches than cream.

"Tell me a little bit about yourself and your background."

I obligingly filled him in on my education and employment history.

"And your family?" he questioned further.

I disliked discussing my parents' accident and my divorce, but since he persisted, I gave him an overview of my personal history, hoping that would suffice. He listened intently, but displayed no reaction.

"I am always scouting to recruit new talent. As I'm sure Rachael has explained to you, I am interested in cultivating an ongoing business relationship with you. I want to publish your first book, and I believe that we can work something out for the future. How do you feel about that?"

Trying to remain guarded, as Rachael had advised, and yet still show enthusiasm was difficult. "I think it would be wonderful if we can work something out," I replied, smiling, and thought to myself that I'd be an easy mark if this were high stakes poker.

Chapter Six

Trey was as good as his word. By the end of the following week, Rachael called with an offer that far exceeded my expectations. There was a hitch, though. Trey would sign me for my next three books, if I agreed to collaborate with him on a pet project of his, a literary magazine. He was assembling a group of writers, young and old, experienced and new, to be ongoing contributors to the magazine. Some would write how-to articles about writing. Others would critique recently published works. Trey felt he needed someone unfamiliar with the business, a fresh view untainted by knowledge of the current trends within the literary world. After meeting me, he decided that I would be perfect for the job. The hitch was that I would have to move to New York. There would be staff meetings to attend, authors to interview, and a column to contribute to for which I would have to work closely with Trey.

My answer was an emphatic no. I could not and would not leave Angie. She was all I had. I needed her and, though she always put up a strong front, I knew she needed me too. It was a once in a lifetime offer, but I couldn't build a career at my sister's expense.

After giving Rachael my final decision, I told Angie that my book had been accepted, but that Trey had made no other offer. I had to get away for a few days for fear Angie might sense I was hiding something, so I planned to tag along with a couple of girls from work to Put-In-Bay for the Labor Day weekend.

The island, in Lake Erie, is one big summer party. Shelly and Mia sat in the front seat of Shelly's little Volkswagen convertible, while I took the backseat, letting the wind blow away my disappointment and depression the whole two hours to Port Clinton. We boarded the Jet Express to Put-In-Bay, and as I scanned the passengers, I realized that I was among the oldest, if not the oldest. Mia was six and Shelly seven years younger than I, but it had never been an issue. I must have been born a decade too soon, or else I was just a late bloomer, I guessed. I had to laugh; at this point I didn't care.

We dropped our bags at Ashley's, a quaint old bed and breakfast, complete with a shaded porch lined with wicker rockers and hanging baskets of pink petunias, and headed on foot to where the action was. Loud music and laughter wafted in the air as we approached the Beer Barrel Saloon on Delaware Avenue, the main drag. It was a far cry from Paris, but it was exactly what I needed.

We drank Long Island Iced Teas, took turns buying rounds of Jell-O shots, ate pizza, and danced till the wee hours of the morning.

Meanwhile, Trey, upset that I had refused his offer, had gotten my phone number from Rachael, hoping that a call from him personally might change my mind. When he had called for me, Angie intercepted and took the opportunity to tell him that she was surprised that Horizon House would not want to snatch me up before another publisher had the chance. Confused, Trey explained that he was eager to sign me, and that he was calling for that very reason, to try to convince me to change my mind and accept his offer.

Angie was sitting on the deck reading the paper when I returned Sunday afternoon. "How was your trip?" she asked casually, her eyes hidden behind sunglasses.

"Great," I said as I plopped onto the lounger, "It was just what I needed, a little time to get crazy. It helped put everything in perspective. What's cooking? Whatever's on the grill smells terrific."

Ignoring my question about supper, she said, "You know what else puts things in perspective? A conversation with Trey," and removing the glasses, she glared angrily at me.

"Trey called?" I asked tentatively.

"Olivia, how could you lie to me about Trey's offer? When I spoke with him, he said, 'Your sister must love you very much to give up so much for your sake.' I felt like a ball and chain holding you back."

"No, no, you should never feel that way. It was as much for me as for you. I don't want to be all alone in New York, and have you all alone here. It's not worth it. It doesn't make sense."

"What doesn't make sense is rejecting an offer to grow and have a career doing what you love. You need to move on with your life, especially after your breakup with Rick. I know how hard it's been on you. A fresh start is just what you need right now. Don't be afraid to reach for the brass ring. I will be here to support you and cheer you on. Don't you see? Your success validates me. Your success is my success."

I ran to her and we held each other tight as tears streamed down our cheeks.

New York was at the same time invigorating and unnerving.

Rachael had insisted I move in with her in her apartment on East Seventy-Ninth Street. Divorced just three months earlier, she was lonely in the spacious three-bedroom apartment and welcomed the company, as well as the additional income. Her ex-husband, a lawyer, had provided a lavish lifestyle, but now things were different, and maintaining that standard of living was difficult. Rachael was forty-five, tough on the surface, but with a heart of gold.

After she left for the office in the mornings, I had the apartment to myself the rest of the day. With her approval, I had turned the spare bedroom into my office where I was beginning work on my next novel. I met with Trey twice a week, once to discuss my progress on the book, and once to compare notes and brainstorm for the magazine. A staff meeting was held every Monday morning at nine.

During my first two weeks in New York, I was so homesick I called Angie twice a day. Adjusting to big city life took time. I missed not having a car. I had to catch a cab or walk everywhere I went. I was too afraid of getting lost, or mugged, to try the subway. And I missed Angie's cooking. Rachael was a terrible cook, I found out. Luckily, she seldom had time to put a meal together. Following Angie's directions, I prepared a few decent dinners, but I discovered that food didn't taste as good when you made it yourself. On the up side, I'd lost seven pounds.

Challenging as life was, I was determined to make a fresh start with my new career. I would forget all my romantic notions about love and finding a special someone to share my life with. I would save those sugary sentiments for my novels. I was going to make a name for myself. I had a talent and my life revolved around my writing from now on. It was just what I needed to forget about Rick. What a paradox, I thought. I was giving up on romance and love when they were the very ideals that had won me the career I'd always dreamed of.

Trey turned out to be unexpectedly warm under that aloof English formality. He was aware that I was having a difficult time adjusting and went out of his way to make things easier. We lunched together at least once a week. His insights and suggestions were very helpful to my writing. He had definitely taken me under his wing, becoming not just my boss, but my mentor.

One Monday morning after our staff meeting, I was stuffing papers into my briefcase as the room emptied, leaving only Trey and me. "So, have you been able to enjoy some of the cultural advantages of living in New York?" he asked.

"Oh yes," I said, "Rachael took me to the Metropolitan Museum of Art last week and Saturday night we went to see *Forty-Second Street* on Broadway," I said enthusiastically.

"Excellent, excellent," he said distractedly. He seemed to be doing an extraordinary amount of paper shuffling. "Well," he proceeded stiffly, "if you haven't plans for this Saturday night, I have tickets for the American Ballet Theater at the Metropolitan Opera. They're performing a compilation of classical and contemporary pieces. I think you would enjoy it." He hadn't looked up, his head still bent over the papers.

Trey's offer surprised me and I wasn't sure how to respond. "It sounds wonderful," I murmured, wondering if this was unusual or merely standard procedure, something he did with all of his new proteges from time to time. I didn't know much about Trey, apart from his literary acumen, except that he was not married. "Who else will be going?" I asked, attempting a nonchalant air.

"Olivia, I am inviting only you." He removed his reading glasses and his eyes were on me in a disarming way. "I want you to expand your knowledge and experience. A writer requires constant stimulation." The panic I was feeling must have surfaced to my face because Trey immediately clarified, "I am referring to cultural stimulation. Please be assured that I have no intention of corrupting you or compromising your values."

"Of course not, I didn't mean to imply...." I stammered, beet-red with embarrassment.

Trey cut in quickly, rescuing me. "Fine, then. I'll pick you up at six-thirty sharp. We'll dine at Le Cirque, before the ballet. In the meantime, get busy on that book, and I'll see you for our regular meetings later in the week." With a curt little nod, he left the room.

That night, while Rachael and I were relaxing over glasses of Chardonnay, I filled her in on my conversation with Trey.

"It's not his MO to take staffers out," she said. "He was involved several years ago with Paula, one of the senior staff members who transferred here from Horizon House's London office. I think their relationship had more to do with them being the only two Brits in the office than having a love connection. Anyway, she transferred back to London, homesick I guess."

"I can certainly understand that," I said. Still, I couldn't help but wonder what was behind his invitation.

Saturday, Trey rang the doorbell promptly at six-thirty. Rachael ushered him in as I put the finishing touches on my makeup. I wore the same little black dress I had worn with Rick. It brought back memories that were still quite painful. It seemed a lifetime ago that Rick and I were together and in love. I was no longer bitter. The times we shared were cherished memories. They were all that I had, other than a few photographs and my ring, which I treasured and wore now in remembrance of the happiest time of my life.

I was walking a tightrope with Trey. He was a kind, intelligent, and generous man, but he was also my boss. The last thing I wanted right now was to get involved in a relationship with any man, let alone one who could fire me. He had said, basically, that he had no ulterior motives, but men were men. I was at a critical point in my career.

Writing had to be my main focus. The next year would make or break my career as an author. I knew I had to tread lightly tonight, but at the same time, lay ground rules for the future.

After a quick prayer that I still have a job at the end of the evening, I went to greet Trey. He rose, smiling warmly as I entered the living room. "Olivia, you look lovely."

"Thank you."

"We had better be going if we want to make our dinner reservation," he said, and we were on our way.

Rachael had been impressed when I had told her we were dining at Le Cirque. "It takes clout to get a reservation there," she informed me.

We were a few minutes late, but the maitre d' was genial with Trey, laughing and talking amiably. I, however, was obviously invisible to him, since he never once made eye contact with me. The secluded corner table we were led to had everything to do with Trey's "clout" and nothing to do with me. He ordered champagne, a bottle of Roederer Cristal, before I could protest. I hadn't had champagne since Paris. When it was poured, he toasted, "To you, Olivia, and to your future success as an author."

I needed to drink to that. "To success!" I said as we clinked glasses.

I was ravenous, since I had been too nervous about the evening to eat anything all day. Now, I devoured my filet of sole without much conversation. Trey made small talk between bites of the lamb chops he had ordered. A faint smirk settled on his face. I bet he's never seen a woman wolf down a dinner so lustily, I thought, ashamed of myself. I daintily dabbed the corners of my mouth with my napkin in an attempt to at least end the meal in a ladylike fashion.

We reached our seats in the opera house just as the house lights darkened. Rick had taken me to my first ballet. From the first moment to the very last, I had been awed by its beauty and grace. The Ohio Ballet had a good reputation, but the American Ballet Theater was perfection, the best of the best.

Afterwards, Trey suggested we stop for a nightcap before he saw me home, but I told him we could have a drink at the apartment. I was anxious to discuss the whole dating situation with him as soon as possible. Once home, I poured us each a brandy. Holding the large round brandy snifter made me feel sophisticated, although I hated the taste of the drink. "The ballet was incredible," I told Trey. "I favor classical ballet, so I enjoyed the pax de deux from *Swan Lake* the most."

"Tell me what's on your mind, Olivia." Trey cut right to the chase.

"Am I that transparent?" I asked guiltily.

"To me, yes. You've been preoccupied the entire evening, so out with it. What is bothering you?"

I shrugged, not knowing how to begin. "Trey, I'm flattered that you're interested enough in me as a writer and as a person to want to look after me and ... spend time with me, but...."

"But you don't think of me in *that* way," he finished for me.

"I don't think of anyone in that way right now. You know better than anyone that I need to focus all my energy on my career for the next year or so. It could be the turning point for me. And I have to admit, I am concerned about crossing the line between business and personal with you."

"To be totally honest, I am attracted to you, Olivia. I cannot deny it. I do understand your concern about our working relationship. I promise you that I will never let our personal relationship interfere with business. I am, after all, a professional and I would not jeopardize my reputation, or yours, in that way.

"You are correct regarding your career. It requires your full attention, but you also need to maintain a balance in your life. I am suggesting that we see each other occasionally. There will be no pressure from me. I will expect no more than your friendship and the pleasure of your company."

I was surprised to see the worried look on his face.

"Will that arrangement be acceptable to you?" he asked with apprehension and a hint of fear in his tone. "Will that ease your mind?"

His obvious concern touched me. Trey cared for me enough to put my needs above his own. "Yes, Trey, that makes me much more comfortable. Thank you." I couldn't help but hug him.

Chapter Seven

Devastated, Rick had paced the room at the Hotel Hermitage, the beauty of the sunrise shimmering over the Mediterranean lost on him. He had checked with the front desk after returning from the Casino in the morning and knew that Olivia was gone. Gone, he realized, for good.

He didn't blame her. He took full responsibility for what had happened. The fact that he had lost control in the Casino proved that he was still addicted. It came as a shocking revelation.

Rick had acknowledged his gambling to be a problem in college. It had started out innocently enough betting on football games; then came basketball and baseball games, followed by the ponies, poker, and backgammon - anything that could be wagered on. Casino gambling had been the last straw. Once he recognized the hole he was digging for himself, he had stopped cold turkey. A man of extraordinary discipline and willpower, he had claimed his life back of his own accord.

In the eight years since, he had not slipped up, not even once. He thought he had kicked the habit completely until Monte Carlo. At first, he had been leery of going to the Casino, but he hadn't wanted to reveal his weakness to Olivia, and since it was in the past, he saw no reason to deprive her of Monaco's greatest attraction.

Rick made no attempt to win Olivia back in the days following their trip. He felt he had no right to ask her to take him back until he had dealt with and conquered his gambling addiction. He had immediately joined the Gamblers Anonymous program. The group had helped him realize that he was addicted for life and could never let his guard down. It was then that he had known he could never expect

Olivia to take him back. He was far too proud to ask the woman he loved to live with his addiction. To Rick, it was no different than asking her to accept him with a terminal disease. He loved her too much to put her in that position.

The dread of possibly running into Olivia forced Rick to make himself scarce at the office. He accepted every travel assignment that came his way, inadvertently establishing a network of business contacts across the globe. This proved to be an excellent career move. He was at the top of his game and Leonard Kistler didn't have enough to offer, so, taking a bold step, he struck out on his own. Partnering up with a college friend who had financial backing, which was the one thing Rick lacked, they started their own business, a management consulting firm. Their aggressive energy, drive, and determination along with their combined business knowledge and contacts propelled them into a successful firm in a relatively short time.

Initially, Rick had concentrated on gaining control of his gambling and advancing his new business, to the exclusion of everything else. He couldn't look at a woman without thinking of Olivia, her soft creamy skin and that smile that radiated her inner beauty, itself a *raison d'être.*

Then abruptly, his attitude changed. Unable to push her out of his mind by avoiding women, he tried the opposite approach, embracing the fairer sex, literally. After not dating for almost a year, he tried quenching his desire for Olivia with a variety of flavors, but to no avail. Blondes with legs to their necks, quirky redheads, and voluptuous brunettes all paraded through Rick's life, in on a whim and out when he came to his senses.

His buddies envied him. Only Ted Griffith, his partner, knew the torment he suffered silently. Ted had tried to convince him to call Olivia, to talk things out, but Rick would have no part of it. Her move to New York had been the final blow. "It's done," he said with finality. "There's nothing to talk about."

Ambition had become Rick's weakness as well as his strength. His unwavering focus on entrepreneurial success resulted in tunnel vision, blurring the other facets of his life. His dating frenzy had eventually calmed; however, he still went through women with a temporary and disposable attitude, just at a slower pace.

With offices in New York, Chicago, Los Angeles, and London, Rick's clients consisted of the creme de la creme of the business world. It was not uncommon for him to attend charity events sponsored by his clients. It was at one such function that Rick met Tiffany.

The charity was a Los Angeles children's hospital specializing in neonatal care; the event was a dinner and silent auction of artworks. Rick was discussing the state of the economy with Gerald Preston, chairman of the board of Preston Investments, Inc., a highly respected investment company and sponsor of the evening, when a striking young woman with a face framed in flaming red pixy hair approached. Flashing a dazzling smile at Rick, she kissed Jerry Preston on the cheek. "Daddy, you haven't introduced me to your friend."

"Maybe because this is the first I've seen you this evening, my dear." Jerry Preston, always direct and to the point, cleared his throat. "Rick, may I introduce my daughter, Tiffany. Tiffany, the man you're batting your eyes at is Rick Sloane, a business associate of mine."

"Oh, Daddy, please, don't embarrass me," but it was obvious she was not the least bit embarrassed.

"My pleasure, Miss Preston," Rick said as he shook her hand. He noticed that she held his hand just a moment longer and squeezed it just a tad tighter than was appropriate before releasing her grip.

"Rick, call me Tiffany," she purred. Her green eyes held an unmistakable allure. She was clearly pampered and temperamental, but Rick found her unbridled aggression oddly appealing.

His exotic good looks and graceful yet confident carriage had captivated Tiffany, as she had eyed Rick from across the room. She had noted that his taste in clothing was flawless and his physicality spoke of a smoldering sexuality barely hidden under the surface. His deep rich voice only enhanced his understated charm.

Jerry Preston cleared his throat again. "If you'll excuse me Rick, I'd better mingle with the others." He hurried off, leaving Rick to fend for himself with his daughter.

"Where have you been hiding? Why haven't I met you before?" Tiffany asked in a sultry whisper.

"I haven't been hiding anywhere," Rick answered plaintively. "Until now, I've always met with your father at his office or mine. This is the first time we've gotten together outside of work."

"We'll have to make sure it isn't the last," she whispered with a flicker of mischief in her eyes, and then quickly added, "What do you say we get out of here?"

Rick was up for the challenge. He had a feeling Gerald Preston knew of his daughter's wanton ways, and wouldn't blame him for accepting her offer. He had made an appearance and spoken to everyone necessary. Ted was there to represent the firm. "What did you have in mind?" Rick replied.

"The beach house in Malibu," she said. "Come on."

Rick had ridden to the charity event with Ted, so Tiffany drove her Mercedes coupe to Malibu. The sun had set less than an hour earlier leaving the sky a deep indigo blue. Stars were abundant in the clear pristine night as the car glided along the coastline. Eventually, they pulled into the U-shaped drive of a beautiful two-story structure with stucco walls and tiled roof. Greenery and flowers of all sorts bordered the drive and walkway to the front door. Inside, the house was done in a comfortable southwestern style. Navajo rugs were strewn over tile floors; beamed ceilings dangled rustic light fixtures; and clay pottery was scattered throughout. The side of the house facing the ocean was almost a solid wall of windows. Glass doors opened onto a deck with steps leading down to the beach.

"Let's go for a swim." Tiffany dropped her purse and keys on the kitchen counter. She was still wearing her cocktail dress of burnt orange, which, with her hair, reminded Rick of a flame flickering in a breeze. Rick was in his suit, the jacket slung over his shoulder.

"I have nothing to wear," he said, glancing down at his clothing.

"Perfect," Tiffany smiled with a glint in her eyes. "Oh, I suppose there's something suitable upstairs."

In minutes, they had changed and were running into the waves. They bobbed and splashed and swam until they emerged from the water refreshed and breathless. The white bikini Tiffany wore fit her reed thin body like a second skin. As Rick wrapped a towel around her shoulders, she leaned into him. She lifted her lips to touch his, lightly at first, then firmly and deliberately seeking satisfaction. When he responded, it was sudden and with great force. Pulling her onto the sand, he peeled the tiny pieces of cloth from her body. She had been teasing him all night. This was what she wanted, he thought, what she had been asking for since they met. He plundered, filled with carnal desire, and she responded, each feeding off the other.

Tiffany had her sights set on Rick and she usually got what she wanted. But Rick was his own man, not about to be led around by the nose by a headstrong, albeit beautiful woman. Their first encounter had led to many more. Rick was seemingly the only one who could tame the tiger in Tiffany. She learned the limits of his temper and adjusted her mercurial temperament accordingly.

They had been seeing each other for three months now, and Rick knew he had to make a decision. Clearly, Tiffany wanted him, not just for the moment, but forever. She was not just any girl. As the daughter of the wealthy and influential Gerald Preston, she had connections that could open doors to the elite clientele Rick needed if he wanted to play in the big leagues. He knew if he dated her much longer and ended up breaking it off, his intentions could be misconstrued as leading her on, and no matter that she was the one prodding the relationship along. He was aware that those same connections that could benefit him could also slam doors in his face. It was a sticky situation.

Rick had flown to Los Angeles on Friday. He would spend the weekend with Tiffany in Malibu and meet with clients out of his LA office the beginning of the week. When he arrived at the beach house at eight, Tiffany was there, ready and waiting. She darted across the room and jumped into his arms wrapping her legs around him and smothering him with kisses.

"Hey, Red, better calm down, I might think you missed me," Rick said, as he broke her hold on him and put her down.

"And you'd be right. You were gone too long. Two weeks is too long," she pouted.

"When duty calls...."

"Well you're here now, and you're all mine," she said, possessively.

"What did you have in mind?" The question was unnecessary. Rick knew precisely what was on her mind - the same thing that was always on her mind - seducing him.

"You know I don't cook, but I did order take-out. We could eat dinner," she paused, her catlike eyes smoldering, "or skip it and nibble on each other."

They were in the great room that overlooked the ocean. The constant rhythm of waves breaking was reassuring and peaceful. A misty rain outside had chilled the air, but flames from the fireplace warmed the room and cast a golden glow.

Tiffany slowly and seductively unbuttoned her white blouse and let it fall open, revealing bare breasts. "See anything that looks tasty?" she whispered in his ear. She loved flaunting her body. Rick had to admit that her bold confidence turned him on. It wasn't long before he was hot and hard and randy. He gave in to the urge she aroused in him.

Later, they dined on smoked salmon, pickled eggs, a fresh, crusty baguette, and brie with a bottle of champagne while Tiffany rattled off all the latest gossip. Rick sat silently for a time, mulling over the news that in a month her parents would be leaving to spend the winter in their home in Venezuela. The clock was ticking in his head. Time was running out. Then casually, almost as an afterthought, he asked, "Should we tell them before or after their trip?"

"What, that we're getting married?" Tiffany quipped sarcastically.

"Yes," was all Rick replied.

Chapter Eight

Time swept away in a whirlwind of meetings, engagements, and work. More than a year had gone by since my move to New York. The promotional tour of *Journey of Love* had been exciting, but draining. I was seeing the business side of being an author. It was not all champagne and roses. It could be tiring and monotonous at times, but it was all worth it. The thrill I felt every time I saw my words and my name in print was indescribable.

I had come to depend on Trey in many ways. As my publisher, his unerring judgment had propelled my novel to the bestseller's list. His guidance and mentoring had helped me improve my craft and grow as a writer. Personally, his kindness and unwavering loyalty had been pivotal in my settling into the New York lifestyle.

Once again, he had been as good as his word. He was attentive and affectionate, without pressing for more. Guilt plagued me since I couldn't reciprocate his feelings. I did have great affection for Trey, but as a friend, not a lover. I probably seemed callous at times, but I didn't want to lead him on. That would be cruel when I knew I couldn't give him the passionate kind of love he deserved. I hoped I would never hurt anyone in that way. I still bore the scars from my own such experience.

New York, dressed in its holiday best with glittering lights and decorations, beautiful window displays, and the giant tree in Rockefeller

Center, was joyous and lively during the Christmas season, but it was not enough to lure me from home. My plans had been set for months. I was going home to Ohio for Christmas and New Year's. Trey was spending the holidays in London with his sister's family.

My flight was scheduled for the afternoon. I met Trey in his office for the last time before my departure. The second novel was progressing nicely and Trey was pleased. "You must relax and forget about work during your holiday," he insisted.

"My sentiments exactly. You should follow your own advice," I admonished.

"Unfortunately, my plans have changed. I was forced to cancel my flight. The magazine is late for printing, so I must stay to proofread copy with the editor," he said, trying to cover his disappointment with a matter-of-fact tone.

"Will you be able to catch another flight?" I knew the answer as I spoke.

"No, all overseas flights have been booked far in advance."

"So what will you do on Christmas?"

"I'm sure I can impose on friends of mine, Colin MacBeth and his wife. They live in the Hamptons. I can drive out to their place for the day."

By now I knew Trey well enough to know he would do no such thing. If he hadn't been invited earlier, he would not think of inviting himself, certainly not at the last minute. He would end up alone in some watering hole that happened to be open. I couldn't stand the thought of it.

"I have a great idea," I announced. "When you've finished here, come to Ohio. Getting a flight shouldn't be that difficult. I'd love you to meet Angie and the rest of my family and friends. They've been dying to meet you anyway. I talk about you so much that they feel like they know you already."

"Thank you, Olivia, but I couldn't interfere with your holiday plans."

I could tell he was weakening.

"Don't be ridiculous!" I took control. "I won't leave you here to be alone on Christmas. Trey, I can't think of anyone I'd rather share my family with than you," and I realized as I spoke that it was true.

Angie and Trey hit it off even better than I expected. She loved that he was mannerly and polite, and the fact that it was not an act. She could see that he was sincerely a gentleman through and through. He fascinated Aunt Rosa, Uncle Louie, and the rest of the family with tales of his childhood in England.

He recounted how he had begun his career in publishing. "I was tall and lanky for my age, and very awkward. My feet seemed to always be in my way, arriving everywhere before I did. It was normal for me to run into things, and if my huge feet weren't wreaking havoc, then my long gangly arms seemed to be in constant motion, spilling food and drinks or tipping lamps, vases, and what-have-you.

"It was no wonder that I was never chosen to play cricket or football, what you call soccer. I knew I needed to find another area in which to excel, so I started writing about the games in the school paper. Eventually, I wrote other articles and editorials, and then became editor-in-chief. Working on the paper was the first thing I could do that came easily and didn't leave me feeling clumsy. So I guess I have my big feet to thank for my career," he finished in his self-depreciating way.

I was pleased to see that my family had succeeded in cracking the stoic shell that usually surrounded Trey.

This Christmas had been the best ever, except for the one with Rick. A barrage of memories of him had been triggered at every turn - our favorite bistro, the park where we played tennis, the movie theater, the ice cream parlor, and the streets where we walked hand in hand.

Coming home had the bittersweet taste of both success and failure.

Chapter Nine

Angie pulled the soft, freshly scented towels from the dryer and folded them neatly, stacking them according to size, as she reminisced about her life. Neat and tidy, she thought, that's how I've lived. Nothing wrong with being organized and clean, she defended. It might have been nice to take some chances though, try something different, but it was not meant to be.

A caregiver most of her life, she never considered raising her little sister to be a burden - a duty maybe, a responsibility - but never a burden. Since her parents' death when she was twenty-one, she had lived vicariously through Olivia. Joyful for every success Olivia achieved, her good-hearted nature had rendered her incapable of jealousy or envy. She only regretted that she would miss seeing Olivia married, and spoiling the nieces and nephews to come.

The lump was cancerous. The doctor said it had spread quickly from her lymph nodes, when he removed the cancerous tissue. Located under her armpit, it had not shown up in mammograms. Radiation treatments and chemotherapy were her only hope. When she had asked for complete honesty, he had estimated she had three to six months.

Telling Olivia was the one thing she didn't know how to face. They were still thick as thieves and phoned back and forth daily. She knew how hard this was going to be on her sister, how much she depended on her. It's time Livie finds her inner strength, the strength I know she has; she will need it now more than ever, Angie thought.

It was March fifth, Angie's birthday. Olivia was distributing plates of cake and ice cream to the family and friends gathered at the house for the occasion. She had heard the fatigue and weakness in Angie's voice lately, and worried that their separation was taking its toll. She had warned Trey from the beginning that if her move to New York proved too taxing on her sister, then the deal was off.

She observed her sister now, her face gray and gaunt, and was overwhelmed with guilt for having left her for so long. She would call Trey first thing in the morning. He would be upset, but having met Angie, she was sure he would understand.

The last of the guests had gone. Angie had put it off long enough. She sipped a cup of tea at the kitchen table, while Olivia put away the last few remnants of the party. It was a cozy room and the apple motif on the curtains and canisters created a cheery atmosphere, but she was impervious to it tonight. She didn't know how to begin. "Livie, sit down with me for a minute, will you?"

"Sure, just as soon as I finish these dishes," Olivia answered, intent on the job at hand.

"This can't wait," Angie said sternly and looked at her sister with pleading eyes.

Olivia sat down across from her sister, suddenly somber and worried, and knew instinctively that bad news was imminent.

"You know I haven't been feeling well, but you don't know the whole story. I've been waiting for you to come home, so I could tell you in person."

Olivia's eyes opened wide with fear. "What is it?" she asked in barely a whisper.

"I wish there was an easy way to . . ."

"What is it?" Olivia broke in, "tell me."

"I have been diagnosed with cancer," Angie said evenly.

"Oh my God! No, Angie, no, are you sure?"

Angie calmly and unemotionally explained the situation, telling her everything, including the doctor's prognosis.

"Oh, Angie!" There were no words. Livie flew to her sister's arms. Her body shook as torrents of tears poured forth. Her worst fear was becoming a reality. Since her parents' fatal accident, she had been terrified that Angie too might be taken from her. She had dreamed horrible nightmares for years after their deaths. Though the locale would change, the subject was always the same – Angie's life would be threatened. Her sister would be in a car, swimming, taking a walk, or even at home when some unknown evil would sneak up on her, overpower her, and start to carry her away. Then Livie would wake up trembling and drenched in sweat, her throat rasping from screams that couldn't escape.

It was a normal reaction, the child psychologist had said. She would outgrow it. And the nightmares did eventually subside, but the paranoia had never completely left her. Now she knew the name of the evil that would take her sister from her.

Hours later, the tears slowed as she sat on the kitchen floor with her head in Angie's lap, her sister's hand smoothing her unruly curls. She could focus only on the present, on the hand gently and comfortingly stroking her head.

Even as I sat at my sister's feet, being lulled into a calm, I knew it was time. Time for me to step up, take charge, and do what had to be done. The time of being cared for and comforted was over. The time of nurturing and comforting had begun.

I won't let Angie down, I swore to myself. I will pull strength from somewhere inside me. I will be her protector, her guardian, as she has been for me. My pain would have to be set aside, take a backseat to Angie's needs and well being. There was no time to feel sorry for myself now. How could I possibly dwell on my own misery when she is the one who is weak, suffering, dying?

It was a role I was unaccustomed to, but I learned gradually, awkwardly, how to manage the household and care for my terminally ill sister, while dealing with my own feelings. Actually, I discovered that if I kept in perpetual motion - nursing, fixing, and fussing - I didn't have time for feeling. By the end of the day, I was too exhausted to think or feel. It was a cowardly, though effective, way to get through each day.

Trey had reacted just as I had guessed, insisting that I take as much time from my work as needed. After inquiring about Angie, his concern had been for me and how I was coping. The distress I felt more than heard in his voice was like an arm around my shoulders, soothing and warming my heart.

The chemotherapy treatments that Angie endured twice a week left her weak and nauseous. Her hair fell out in clumps. I bought her a variety of hats and scarves, which I too wore at times, so she wouldn't feel conspicuous. I did my best to keep a positive attitude, but her condition was deteriorating. She was slowly dying before my eyes. I had never felt so helpless or useless. Making soup and fluffing pillows were superfluous gestures against this fierce enemy.

When she had a spell where she couldn't breathe, I called 9-1-1 and she was transported to the hospital. I stayed with her day and night and ran home only to shower and change clothes, while my aunt or uncle filled in. Hooked up to tubes and equipment that did who knows what, Angie fell in and out of consciousness, eventually more out than in. I kept my vigil by her side, not understanding why this had to happen, but praying, if she could not be healed, that she be spared any more pain and suffering.

A few days later, my prayers were answered. It was six or so in the morning. I was asleep in the chair next to her bed, when I heard my name. I jumped at the sound, weak as it was, and leaned over the bed. I held her hand in mine, and gently smoothed her forehead. "I'm here, Angie. It's okay. I'm here with you," I whispered to her.

"Livie, you'll be strong, won't you? I want you to live life and be happy. For me, will you?" The words came hard for her.

"Angie, don't think about that now. Just rest."

"No, promise me," she insisted.

"I promise, Angie, I promise."

She drew enough strength to squeeze my hand, and then all went limp.

Trey and Rachael flew in from New York for the funeral. Roy willingly served as pallbearer. Neighbors, family, and friends brought hams and chicken, pizza and pasta, and desserts of all kinds to the house. I knew that they meant well, that it was a gesture of kindness and sympathy, but in the midst of the grief, I couldn't understand how they thought food would heal the ache in my chest, the emptiness and loss. It was like taping a Band-Aid on a gunshot wound.

In the following weeks, I handled the paperwork, dealt with the bank, the insurance company, and the lawyers. I paid bills, had mail forwarded to my New York address, and closed up the house. I didn't know if I would keep it or sell, but I couldn't deal with that right now.

I had no idea how I would go on, but life went on whether I was ready for it or not. Gradually, the pain of losing Angie settled into a constant dull ache in my chest. For months after returning to New York, I lived a rote existence, day in and day out shoving one foot in front of the other, merely going through the motions of living.

One sun-filled afternoon, in an attempt to shake my dismal mood, I took a walk in Central Park. I watched children play, dogs chase, and joggers run. Angie's words echoed in my mind, "I want you to live life and be happy." She would be angry if she saw me now, disappointed, I thought. I just wished I could be happy. And as I walked, I began to feel stronger, invigorated, and, as though she was listening and granting my wish, the weight of my grief became less and less. Gradually, it seemed to be lifted from my shoulders. I kept on, faster and further. On and on I marched until, late in the afternoon, I eventually collapsed on a park bench from sheer exhaustion. With a clearness of mind, I realized that surviving my greatest fear, agonizing as it was, turned out to be very freeing. The worst thing that could possibly have happened to me had happened, and in the greater scheme of things there was nothing left to fear. The loss of my sister had proven to be a life-altering experience for me. I came out of this hideous tragedy armed with a strength I had no idea I possessed.

Chapter Ten

I threw myself into my work with a vengeance. The agony and loss I had experienced brought my writing to life and gave it a depth it had lacked. Characters took on new dimensions. Descriptions were vivid and concise. I wrote as though my senses were on fire.

The last few years of total commitment to my work had paid off. I had become a success, critically and financially. I received accolades and awards for my writing. I was on the upper crust's A-list and garnered invitations to all the right parties. My career was booming and I could pretty much call the shots, but my personal life was in shambles. When I allowed myself to feel at all, I was guarded, at best, by the walls I had built around me.

I had followed Rick's rising star in the business world. Friends and contacts kept me apprized of his progress - the start of his own firm, the opening of each new office. Articles in the newspaper documented his power plays. The society section had covered his marriage and divorce. Now, as one of the most eligible bachelors, his social life was fodder for gossip columns. I followed his life intently, but always from afar.

News of Rick's marriage had hit me hard. Standing in the express line at the grocery store, I was leafing through a magazine when I saw Rick pictured with Tiffany. They were exiting a church. The caption read, "Rick Sloane and Tiffany Preston - a match made in heaven or the board room?"

My lips began to tingle with numbness and then for a second, everything went black. I was conscious and still standing in line when things came back into focus and I saw the cashier staring at me with a strange look on her face. Her lips were moving, but no sound registered. Finally, she grabbed my arm, "Ma'am, Ma'am, are you all right?"

"What?" I looked at her blankly.

"Twenty-four thirty-seven, ma'am," she said, showing signs of impatience.

I paid her and fled the store. At home I heaved in the bathroom till there was nothing left, and then sat in quiet shock on the sofa for an interminable length of time while the room slowly darkened around me. It wasn't until I went to the kitchen for water that I realized I had left the grocery bags at the checkout.

It had been over for a long time, but his marriage gave our relationship the finality it had lacked. Rick's divorce several years later proved to be anticlimactic compared to the fact that he had been able to marry. That the marriage had not worked seemed somehow insignificant.

Matt Jennings, Rick's neighbor and a classmate of mine from Ohio, was now chief financial officer of Rick's firm. He worked out of the firm's New York office, and had looked me up when he made the move. We kept in touch, meeting for lunch or dinner every few months. It was from him that I learned that Rick had not read *Journey of Love*, our love story, until recently, the topic too raw before then.

Rick and I both had come to accept our lives as they were. We were very fortunate really. Each of us had achieved success doing what we enjoyed. We led full lives. We lived well and had the freedom that money allows, yet neither of us had found any happiness that could compare with what we had shared. Nothing and no one had replaced the love we had for each other.

I had so feared running into Rick that I was careful to check out the guest list of any gathering or party I attended in New York. Several times I had had close calls, but was able to diffuse the situation with excuses, and escape before a confrontation took place. Rick, according to Matt, purposely spent most of his time in his other offices, visiting New York only when business required it.

In spite of our efforts to avoid each other, the inevitable occurred. The day was teeth-chattering cold, the wind sweeping a storm in from the northwest. Trey had insisted on taking me to lunch at the Four

Seasons as a special treat. We were seated in the Grill Room with its rich rosewood paneling and magnificent high ceilings. The restaurant was crowded with holiday shoppers, since the Christmas season was in full swing.

After a lovely lunch, topped off with a frothy cappuccino, it was time to get back to work. Trey helped me on with my coat and just as we were leaving, Rick walked through the door. Our eyes met and locked. His registered surprise for a second, then dark as coal, they twinkled with genuine pleasure. On impact, my eyes melted into his, until I caught myself and cooled with a frosty stare. My face, open book that it is, revealed shock and confusion until I gritted my teeth and ordered myself to get a grip or risk looking like a complete fool. This was it - the moment I had both dreamed of and dreaded.

"Olivia, it's good to see you. You look fantastic," Rick said, charm dripping off of every word.

His deep voice resonated in my ears.

Trey cleared his throat, my cue that introductions should be made. Willing myself into control with a proper smile and my best etiquette, I accepted Rick's warm greeting. "Hello, Rick," I said, trying hard to sound nonchalant. "May I introduce William Osborne of Horizon House Publishing? Trey, this is Rick Sloane. He owns the well-known consulting firm of the same name."

"Yes, of course, my pleasure indeed," Trey said, graciously extending his hand to Rick. "Please, call me Trey."

Rick responded congenially and the two men shook hands, silently sizing each other up. Rick's gaze returned to me and I self-consciously made excuses for a speedy departure. Through it all, I hid under a veil of civilized propriety, except for that first moment when our eyes had met and locked for what seemed like infinity.

Once again I hadn't slept a wink. The flight to London was smooth and uneventful, just the way I liked it. Even so, I couldn't rest. Trey had dozed, waking to check on me and keep me company, then nodding off again. I didn't mind. Spending Christmas with him had been his idea. My feelings were mixed. The thought of going home to an empty house, a house without Angie, made me shiver, but it couldn't be avoided forever. And the rest of the family was there. Not this year, I told myself. I will face it, but not just yet. I had planned on staying in New York for the holidays, but Trey had arranged the trip and every detail, surprising it on me the week before. He seemed so excited, and I figured that it might be good for me.

Since my encounter with Rick, flashbacks of the past appeared in my mind more and more often, and without warning. Seeing him again had fanned a spark that I thought had been extinguished years ago. The look in his eyes had left an unsettling, bewildering feeling with me, one that, so far, I had not been able to shake. I was hopeful that a change of scenery would help me put the whole incident in perspective.

Damp and dreary, it was typical English weather, Trey confirmed, with the light drizzle just enough to require intermittent windshield wipers as we left Heathrow Airport and drove into the countryside.

We were on our way to Trey's family home outside of Kent. The rolling green hills, interrupted by an occasional village of stone row houses, church, and pub provided a welcome contrast to the concrete jungle that was New York. I sat quietly, the rural setting already working its magic to calm my frayed nerves. The green of the hills dotted with flocks of sheep smelled of freshness and nature and peace.

We turned off the two-lane road and were on a narrow pavement that wound through thick woods. Eventually, it opened out to a wide lawn flowing to the edifice of a magnificent stone mansion. Wide steps with stone lions guarding each side rose to gigantic wooden doors, each flanked by huge pots brimming with greenery.

"Treyyy?" I said, at once questioning and accusing.

"Olivia, welcome to Osborne Manor, my family home," he said, trying to sound cavalier, but the pride came through.

"Trey, you never told me . . . I wasn't prepared for, for . . . this," I said, with a sweep of my hand. I hadn't known what to expect, hadn't thought about it really. Nothing this grand had even crossed my mind.

The last word had barely passed my lips when one of the huge wooden doors swung open and three children between the ages of three and seven, I guessed, came running out laughing and shouting "Uncle Trey! Uncle Trey!" down the steps to the car. Trey came round and helped me out as they reached him with excited hugs and kisses. One by one, he acknowledged each by name, greeting them with the loving warmth of a doting uncle.

Trey's sister Stella and her husband Roger, had followed the children. They made a handsome couple - tall, slim, and erect. The lord and lady of the manor, I thought, briefly considering if I should curtsy. Too many Jane Austen novels, I decided. Trey introduced me, and then he and Roger brought our bags as Stella walked with me into the house. "I'm glad you could come. Trey is so fond of you. I'm happy we finally meet." She said it openly and without affectation.

My face flushed, matching the poinsettias lining the foyer. What had he told them about us, I wondered uneasily? Then silently chastising myself for overreacting, I said, "Thank you for having me. I had no idea Trey's family home was so grand."

Stella showed me to my room on the second floor. I couldn't help exclaiming with oohs and ahs of delight when she opened the door to the beautifully appointed room done in a warm peach tone. "My favorite color," I explained.

Trey and Roger caught up with us, delivering my suitcases to the room. "Everything okay?" Trey asked.

"Fine," I smiled. "I'll deal with *you* later."

"It's three now. We'll have cocktails at six, dinner at seven. You must be tired and jet-lagged. It might be a good time for a nap," Stella suggested.

"That's a great idea. See you later." I closed the door, leaned against it, and let my eyes roam this new paradise that was mine for now. The room, cheerful and warm, had tall windows overlooking a terrace with gardens that trailed down to a creek meandering its way across the property. The walls, covered in peach silk, met the high ceiling with ivory crown molding. The bed, which dominated the room, was a massive four-poster topped with a fluffy duvet colored with cream roses opening to reveal peach centers, matching the window dressings.

In the far corner, a lounger was situated next to one of the leaded windows, the small table next to it stacked with books for light reading and a bowl of fresh fruit. A vase of roses matching those on the fabric, from the estate's greenhouse I discovered later, adorned the dresser. I could stay here forever, I thought wistfully, as I undressed and climbed under the covers.

I awoke in time to enjoy a leisurely bubble bath in the adjoining bathroom, stocked with candles, more flowers, and a bottle of bubbly. I hadn't been pampered like this in a long time and I intended to enjoy every minute of it.

Not sure how formal dinner was to be, I dressed in a gray wool sheath with the single strand of my mother's pearls. I followed the sound of voices to the living room. A Christmas tree a good ten feet tall trimmed in red and gold glittered brightly. Trey and Roger were already into a discussion of politics. Trey broke off as I entered the room and came to greet me with a kiss on the cheek. "You look amazing, Livie." He'd just recently relaxed from calling me Olivia.

"A nap helped, but I think it was the bubbles, for bathing and drinking, that really did the trick."

"I'll have to remember that," he said with a wink. Normally, such a comment would have set off an alarm in me, but I was too relaxed to take notice.

Stella joined us a few minutes later, having gotten her brood settled down for the night, and we all toasted the holidays and each other. Shortly thereafter, we filed into the dining room, which was festively decorated with garlands of fresh pine and pots of poinsettias. The conversation was animated and cheerful as we dined at the enormous table on Beef Wellington and, for dessert, Black Forest Cake. Afterwards, we retired to the study for coffee and brandy. Stella embarrassed Trey by recounting stories of their childhood, the trouble they got into, and the way her big brother had protected and looked after her.

It was the best time I'd had in ages. Trey's sister and brother-in-law were very down-to-earth, unpretentious people, despite their lavish surroundings. Trey himself was livelier, more light-hearted than I had ever seen him.

During the week that followed, the weather cleared and we walked the gardens, dormant now, and peaceful. Mounting horses from the stables, we rode wooded paths to open fields, feeling the lay of the land. We visited the cathedral in Kent, and I shopped in local stores for Christmas gifts for everyone. We played with the children, and took them to the movies. In my dreamy room, I rested and read, a treat I rarely had the opportunity to enjoy in New York.

Christmas Eve came quickly. The manor filled with guests, friends and family of the Osbornes. Luckily, Trey had advised me to pack an evening gown "just in case." I had chosen a close-fitting gown of burgundy velvet gathered at one shoulder. I wore my hair swept up, and added my usual touch of sparkle with chandelier earrings.

As I descended the grand staircase, a string quartet played, their music mingling with the laughter in the air. Trey's eyes sparkled with excitement and, dare I say, pride as he introduced me to other family members, friends, old school chums, and several business associates. His arm was around me most of the evening in an unmistakably proprietary manner. I surprised myself by not only allowing it, but also enjoying the hint of intimacy in the gesture.

I considered myself an astute judge of character, but I found myself marveling at this man I thought I knew so well. At home and in his element, Trey was overflowing with enthusiasm, wit, and charm. Personality exuded from every pore. Like watching a picture take on three dimensions, he had come to life. The quiet and proper mannerisms remained, but now there was a dynamic, elegant, almost regal quality in his movements, his carriage, even his voice. He had always been confident in his work and knowledge of the business, in his understated, cool style. This was different. He was for once wearing the power that confidence breeds on the outside for all to see. It was intoxicating. It was sensual. It was sexy.

We danced in the ballroom, Trey expertly whirling me around the floor as he smiled into my eyes. I was dizzy and lightheaded from dancing, or was it something else, as he led me out to the glass-encased sunroom, lit only by the lights of the ballroom behind and the glow of the moon above. Trey saw that the chill of the unheated room brought goose bumps to my arms, and in one easy fluid motion he pulled me to him. Before I could find my voice, he spoke. “Can’t you feel it, Livie, how perfect we are for each other?” he said in a throaty whisper. He tightened his grip on my arms, as he caught my eyes levelly. The room vibrated with tension. In his eyes shone deep pools of passion. “Can you honestly say you can’t feel it?”

Everything about him was compelling, mesmerizing. A thrill fluttered through me; breath came in gasps.

“I’ve waited, but I will be put off no longer. I love you, Olivia. I want to marry you.” Then his lips were on mine, forcefully taking what he had wanted for so long. My protests were smothered. He took me in boldly, undaunted by my resistance, until I relented, at first in resignation, then in response to the longing he had unleashed. All thought dissolved into sensation. The hunger in me that had gone unsatisfied for years surfaced with an unquenchable appetite.

As suddenly as he had begun, he stopped, holding me out from him. Darkness shadowed his aristocratic features as he gazed solemnly into my eyes. “You must decide. Soon,” he warned. Then, he rubbed my arms with warmth, and his face and tone lightened. “Let’s get back in. You’re freezing,” and with a kiss on the forehead he guided me inside.

Chapter Eleven

For the third time I hit the snooze button and pulled the covers over my head. I didn't want to wake up. That would mean I'd have to think about everything that had happened and I wasn't ready to face it today, maybe tomorrow.

Since Christmas Eve and Trey's ultimatum, I could think of little else. We had referred to the whole episode only once, on the flight back to New York. He had held my hand in his, searching my eyes for an answer. Never unreasonable, he would give me a chance to digest and consider his proposal, but, and he was very firm, he wouldn't wait forever. I knew how hard it had been on him these past years to hold his feelings in check and not press the issue. He wouldn't take it any longer. I respected him for taking a stand.

When I tried to sort things out, it all ended up swirling around in my head blending together, fading into a blur until nothing was clear. I wished I could let it all swirl down the drain with my bath water as I forced myself to prepare to meet the day. What a wimp I am, I thought. Sure it was easier to crouch and hide from life at times, but what good does that do? Better to meet life head on, I persuaded myself, not very convincingly, and made a mental note to never attempt motivational speaking.

In reality, the only choice to be made was whether or not to marry Trey. Rick, of course, was not an option. I was aware of that, but in the interest of being fair to Trey I had to consider my feelings for Rick. I couldn't accept one man's proposal simply because another's wasn't forthcoming. It was done every day, I knew, but not by me. Settling was not the way to enter into a marriage. I was sensible enough to realize it would be unfair to all and disastrous in the end.

Just reason things out, I thought. Put things in the simplest terms. Follow the truth. Truth was I had feelings for two men. One was the good guy, all but wearing a white hat. Attractive, understanding, patient, he had always been there for me in times of need. He was intelligent, fiercely loyal, and, just recently known to me, passionate. He was real, a stand-up guy whom you could count on.

I realized that I had taken him for granted. How would I feel if I lost him? Devastated, lost, afraid. He was my best friend. I had not thought of him romantically until that magical night, but there was no denying he had set me on fire. I was still shocked by his passion and my response to it. I shook my head in amazement at the very thought.

Then there was the guy in black. Nothing but heartache and pain. Not true, I corrected myself. Stick to the facts. In truth, he had given me the greatest joy, the purest sense of happiness I had ever felt. Smooth, sensual, breathtaking, he was a roller coaster ride with dizzying downward spirals and heart-throbbing peaks. He was passion in a package - exciting, handsome, and hot. But, apparently without much staying power. In a snap, he had disappeared. The memory of him lingered like a scent in the air - invisible, untouchable, but undeniable.

An easy choice, my mind decided. The writing was on the wall. Trey was the better choice, the right choice. But why didn't my heart concur with my mind? Why wasn't I happy and relieved that I had reached a decision, a logical decision? Instead, I felt uneasy, unsettled. It made no sense. I wished I could control my life and the people in it as easily as I manipulated the characters in my books, with a stroke of the keyboard.

Life was a journey, not a destination, my mother used to say. I supposed it was the navigating, the daily living of it that made all the difference. Trey may not give me the exciting twists and turns that took my breath away, but he was straight and steady and definitely in for the long haul. And I loved him. The threat of losing him had proven that to me without a doubt.

Three dozen of my favorite roses were delivered to the apartment on Valentine's Day. Trey had made dinner reservations for eight o'clock at Le Perigord, but I had asked him to meet me at the Empire State Building, explaining that I had to deliver some papers to my lawyer's office first. Then I suggested we meet on the observation deck on the hundred-and-second floor. "It'll be fun," I coaxed, "and if I'm late at least you'll have a view."

He found it odd, but humored me. He was aware of my hopelessly romantic outlook on life, and realized that meeting on the observation deck of the Empire State Building on Valentine's Day was a re-creation of the movie, *An Affair to Remember.*

I didn't spot him standing off to the side of the elevator. I walked to the edge of the deck, overlooking the lights of Manhattan, as I scanned the small group of people braving the wind and cold. Trey came up behind me, "Looking for someone?" he asked, smiling and handsome in his trench coat.

I turned to him. He had given me the perfect opening. "Yes," I smiled back. Gazing into his eyes, I went on, with all the sincerity and love I felt. "I've been looking for someone for a long time and I've finally found him. Yes, Trey, I mean, William Henry Osborne the Third, I will marry you."

For the first time, I saw tears well up in Trey's eyes. He pulled me close and kissed me deeply. Then, to my surprise, digging into his pocket he pulled out a tiny box, opened it, and held it out to me. "Please accept this ring as a sign of my love."

"Oh! Oh! Oh, Trey!" was all I could stutter.

He placed the sparkling ring on my finger. It was a huge oval sapphire encircled with diamonds in a platinum princess setting.

"It's magnificent!" I whispered in awe.

"It's been in the family for a century or so," he said modestly.

Finally finding my voice, I asked him, "How did you know?"

"Darling, I know you better than you think. Why else would you have me meet you atop the Empire State Building on Valentine's Day?" he said, laughing.

"I hate being a foregone conclusion," I pouted.

He shook his head. "Believe me, Livie, you were never that!"

Chapter Twelve

His experience with Tiffany had taught Rick that the ease with which he and Olivia got along, the affection that flowed naturally between them, the love they shared, were rare and precious gifts, not to be discarded as though easily replaced. Since their chance encounter, he had thought of nothing else.

Half a dozen times he had permitted himself the solitude and comfort of a night savoring a bottle of Johnnie Walker and memories of her. He pictured the devilish twinkle in her eyes when she teased him, and lingered over that smile that lit his world like the sunrise. He remembered the thrill of knowing the pleasure he gave her. Never would he stop blaming himself for losing control, for allowing a sick habit to rob him of her, of everything that mattered. Even if she could have forgiven him and taken him back, he had not been able to forgive himself.

Rick had accepted his fate and learned to live with it - until the moment their eyes had met. In that moment, he drank her in with a thirst only she could quench. He had been shaken by the stirrings seeing her had caused in him. Unable to eat, or sleep, or concentrate, he realized with certainty that he would never be satisfied without her. He would not rest until Olivia was his once again.

The decision was made. Now he had to make it happen. He had to find a way to see her. Within minutes, Rick was on his cell phone with Matt Jennings. He knew Matt kept in touch with Livie. Matt gave him a rundown of her schedule, at least what he knew of it. She was in the office Monday, Wednesday, and Friday mornings for meetings, then lunch, and back to the office to catch up on email, snail mail, and the like, and later she usually took a run in Central Park before heading back to her apartment.

Perfect, Rick thought. He had started a regimen of lifting when he hit thirty, and added running a year ago. Now at thirty-four, his physique was muscular and toned. Running into Livie in the park would be the perfect coincidence. He wished he could approach her head-on, call or go to her apartment, but he knew she would recoil if directly confronted. It would have to seem by chance and unplanned if he were to succeed.

Rick chose a Friday afternoon. With the week all but over, and the weekend just ahead, Rick hoped Olivia would be in a good mood, relaxed and carefree. Matt had been key in finding out her usual route, and afterward, had suffered pangs of guilt for his part in setting her up, but a pair of tickets to see the Yankees from the firm's loge did wonders to ease his pain.

Crisp and clear, yellow with sun, the April day coated Manhattan with springtime. Crocuses bloomed; trees were pregnant with buds as Olivia started her run in Central Park. Pacing herself, she jogged along her normal route around the reservoir. Running had helped her release tension and stress after Angie's death. It replaced the fatigue of grief and angst with a healthy physical exhaustion, and gave her an opportunity to be outdoors. She felt light on her feet today. The sun was shining; it was spring; and she was engaged to be married. It doesn't get much better than this, she mused.

Rick spotted her as she wound her way along the path. He gave her a ten-minute head start, as his stride was much longer and faster, and then took off behind her. He ran at a good clip until she was in sight. Then, with his heart pounding like a bass drum in his chest, he jogged the final yards between them. "Hey," he panted, coming up next to her, "I thought that was you. I'd know that mop of tawny curls anywhere."

The jolt of seeing him so close and casual, in nothing but a T-shirt and shorts, winded her to a dead stop. Without the formality of business attire and propriety to hide behind, as she had on their first encounter, she panicked. She bent down as though to fix her shoe, trying to pull herself together. Furious that he had such an effect on her, she stalled; "My shoe, something in my shoe."

Delighted and encouraged to find her so flustered, Rick pressed on. "You look great, Olivia," he said, and meant it. She was thinner than he had ever seen her, her skin iridescent, her eyes dark, deep, and dangerous. A man could drown in them, he thought. "I didn't know you ran."

"There's a lot you don't know about me," she said with an arrogant flip of her head.

"I'm sure that's true. Why don't we sit down and you can fill me in?"

"I'd love to," she lied, "but I've got to get back."

"It's a beautiful day. What's the rush?"

Reaching for an excuse to get away, she blurted, "My fiancé is waiting."

Now it was Rick's turn to be jolted. She saw his face go pale and immediately her heart ached for him - for her - for anyone suffering life's wicked twists and turns. For anyone suffering life's wicked twists and turns. With a quick recoup, he stepped back and nodded, "Congratulations. I didn't know."

"As I said, there's a lot you don't know about me," she said, still an edge to her voice. She could not excuse his absence during Angie's illness. He hadn't known, of course, until it was too late, but she considered that his fault. He would have known if . . . It didn't matter now, she reminded herself. "Goodbye Rick," she said, her eyes lowered, and she took off in a sprint.

She said it with such finality that Rick's rippling shoulders sagged along with his confidence. He stood, eyes glued to her retreating figure till she vanished from sight. And still he stood, gazing at what was no longer, with eyes narrowed and lips pursed, for an interminable length of time.

Suddenly and with great thrust, he punched the air with a fisted arm and exclaimed victoriously, "Yes!" Deeply attune to Olivia and knowing her better than she knew herself, he realized in that moment that she was not running to someone, but away from him. And that made all the difference.

Rick knew he had a chance. It was a long shot, but he had a chance. As far as he was concerned, it was all he needed. He wanted Olivia back and he would find a way to rekindle her love. When confronted, she had run from her feelings for him. He had to corner her, make her acknowledge those feelings, and soon. This time he would not take no for an answer.

He contrived a plan to bring them together.

Liberty United Bank, a client of his, had been looking for a way to improve public relations. Rick was aware that Horizon House Publishing did all of its banking with Liberty. He recommended to Liberty's Board of Trustees that they sponsor and host a charity event. This would serve several purposes. Sponsoring a charity event is always good PR, and if it were posh enough, it would attract the international clientele the bank was targeting. They, in turn, would pique the interest of the news media, and voila, widespread publicity would be guaranteed.

It was fairly easy for Rick to sell the Board on the idea. More difficult was convincing the bank to locate the event in Monte Carlo, but Rick had an excellent track record and reputation. His advice held weight. It was what they paid him for. He explained that if they wanted international business, they must create an international presence. Monte Carlo would be the perfect venue for the lavish affair, he insisted, sighting its reputation as the undisputed Capitol of the Riviera and the gathering place of the glitterati. Without further discussion, they agreed.

The president of the bank had lost his wife to breast cancer several years ago, and Rick's recommendation that the money raised from the gala be donated to research for finding a cure for breast cancer was well received.

From a purely business standpoint, choosing breast cancer research would enable Liberty United's PR department to put a personal spin on the media coverage of the event. They could sight the loss of one of their own and depict the bank not as a cold, calculating establishment, but rather a feeling, caring organization that was willing to invest in the health and welfare of its people.

Rick was friendly with several top executives of Horizon House and they owed him. He contacted them, pointing out that being represented at the gala by several writers would be beneficial to all, and named Olivia specifically. They got the drift.

The plan was in place. The rest, Rick knew, would be up to him.

Chapter Thirteen

My fury had not subsided even after running the whole way home from the park, stopping midway just long enough to catch my breath. A cool shower had done nothing to cool me down. I paced the apartment like a caged animal, snarling epithets, pounding and striking the air around me. How dare he affect me this way! I was over him. I had meditated, medicated, analyzed, and philosophized over our breakup. I had moved on. Look at all I had achieved - career, fame, and fortune - beyond the scope of my most ambitious fantasies. I was engaged to a wonderful man who loved me. So why, after all the time that had passed, had my pulse raced when he was next to me? Why had my cheeks burned, my mind fogged? It wasn't fair. I had worked hard to get over Rick, and I was over him, damn it, I was.

Above all, I realized that it would be a betrayal of Trey to entertain such feelings. I wouldn't allow it, no matter what the cost. I would rationalize my way out of these notions, mind over matter. As always, I turned to my writing for an outlet, an escape valve to deal with my emotional overload.

Trey was amazed at the progress I'd made on my third novel. At the same time, he noticed the dark hollows under my eyes and an edgy nervousness unusual to my nature.

"I'm just a little tired," I assured him.

"I have good news. I think it's just what you need."

"Don't keep me in suspense. What is it that I need so badly?" I said distractedly, as I fell onto the couch in his office.

"A rest. You've clearly been working long and hard. A trip to the Riviera, Monte Carlo to be exact."

"Sounds like you're the one who's been working too hard. What in the world are you talking about?"

"Horizon House has received invitations to a charity gala being sponsored by Liberty United Bank. It's being held in Monte Carlo the end of May. It's going to be the event of the season. I have been given specific orders that two of our writers are to attend. You are to represent the fiction group and Katherine Porter the nonfiction."

Realizing he was serious, I sat up straight. "What? Monte Carlo?" I said in disbelief. "Oh no, I can't."

"Of course you can. It will be a great opportunity for you. Lots of top names. Loads of publicity. I only wish I could go with you, but I have meetings regarding the buyout of a smaller company that we're considering. They can't be postponed."

Was the whole world on a mission to make my life miserable? I had worked myself into a practically comatose state to avoid thoughts of Rick since that day in the park. Now I was being sent to Monte Carlo, the last place Rick and I had been happy together, the place where I had, for a moment in time, experienced the most passionate love of my entire life. And to top it off, Trey, dear sweet Trey, who had no idea of the memories Monte Carlo held for me, was the one instigating the trip.

"Trey, I won't go without you. Besides, I have too much work to do. It's been going well. I don't want to break my train of thought. I'll go to another charity event here in the city, with you."

"Livie, my dear, I would love to, but this was not my decision. It came directly from the president's office. There's really nothing I can do except contact my friends at Liberty United. They're good people. I'll ask them to look out for you. Why are you so upset? What is it?"

"Oh, nothing really," I backed off. "It's just a surprise. I wasn't expecting it. And I don't like leaving you." It was true, I thought. I didn't like the idea of going to Monte Carlo alone to face all those memories, good and bad.

When I heard that the money raised by the gala would be donated to the research of breast cancer, I stopped arguing. It was a cause very close to my heart. Angie would want me to go, I thought, and facing those memories might be the final step I needed to take to rid myself of the unsettling feelings seeing Rick had brought on. I hoped that revisiting Monte Carlo would put an end to my turmoil and confusion, and allow me to close the book on that part of my life.

Deftly, I drifted through the weeks before the trip, quietly introspective. More than once Trey had caught me staring off into space, preoccupied with the past. My normally light-hearted spirit gave way to moody lapses of silence.

Matt Jennings called, inviting me to lunch. It was a convenient way to find out if Rick planned on attending the gala. When I discreetly mentioned the event, Matt put my concern to rest, clamoring that Rick was involved in a huge merger and was spending his time in his Chicago office.

On the day of my flight, Trey insisted on driving me to the airport and waiting with me in the terminal until departure. As we said our good-byes, he asked me for the hundredth time if I was all right, and for the hundredth time I assured him that I was. His eyes roamed my face searching for a clue that would explain my aloofness, but he found nothing other than a weak smile under eyes heavy with trepidation. He held me close, whispering that he missed me.

I understood that in the past weeks I had been distant. "I know," I shrugged wearily; "I need to get this over with."

In an unsteady voice, he murmured, "Come back to me," and I knew that, although it remained unspoken, he recognized that I was battling my own demons.

Nice was aglow with warm sunshine when we arrived. I had hoped to disguise my mood in the dark clouds of a gloomy rain, but no such luck. The excuse that I wasn't feeling well had explained away my mood during the flight, but now I could see that Katherine was becoming suspicious. As she drove along the coast, gushing over its beauty, I was already awash with memories, drowning in images of my last visit to the Riviera.

I had ignored the information packet that we'd been given, so when she mumbled something about getting lost trying to find the Hotel Hermitage I cringed, and then gave her directions to it. We arrived at the hotel without delay. It was just as I remembered.

Luckily, our rooms were on different floors and I let out a sigh of relief as I closed the door behind me. The room was not large, but adequate. French doors opened to a small balcony with a view of the Mediterranean, just like ours had back then. We weren't meeting for dinner until seven, so I had time to peel off the facade I had hidden behind all day and deal with the memories that were bombarding me.

I replayed the scene from five years ago, every detail as vivid as if it were yesterday - my Paris dress, Rick in his tuxedo, the clean male smell of him. I could still hear his deep voice on the balcony professing how he needed me, wanted me, and loved me. A sigh caught in my chest as the picture was shattered by the memory of what came later - the casino and his harsh demand for money. I stood on the balcony reliving those moments, hoping that doing so would finally rid me of the lingering illusions that haunted me. I had accepted the trip, believing that it was a sign. It was the opportunity I needed to clear my heart and my soul of the past, so that I could look forward without reserve to a future with Trey.

I soaked in the tub and allowed myself the luxury of entertaining every memory of Rick. Now was the time to face them once and for all. I paraded the montage of memories before me, hoping that they were marching into the past to find their place with the rest of my life's experiences.

This evening's dinner would be followed by several speeches, and then the party would reconvene in the Casino for drinks, dancing, and gambling, as desired. Representing Horizon House Publishing, I had to make an appearance at the Casino, but my plan was to escape after I had mingled sufficiently, leaving Katherine with a group of writers from other publishing houses. I was sure she wouldn't miss me, since we hadn't exactly hit it off anyway.

She wrote books on finance: how to budget your spending, how to get out of credit card debt, how to become a millionaire. She had no qualms about giving me her opinion of romance novels - silly, trite, a waste of time - and implied that her work was far more important, writing of things people really needed. She had flaunted this haughty attitude until I was recognized in the airport and a small crowd had gathered for autographs, pushing her aside. Afterward, my only comment had been that apparently people had needs beyond financial that my books attempted to meet.

The gown I had bought for the occasion was purposely splashier than my taste generally ran, but I knew most of the guests were from the world of glamour. And I was allowing for the fact that I might hide my somber mood under the cover of a red dress with plunging neckline and crystal beads. The effect, I thought ruefully, was bold and stunning. Too bad it would be wasted on paparazzi.

It was a shame, too, that the many courses of the elegant dinner were wasted on me. I had no appetite. Even the chocolate-covered strawberries held no appeal.

Suffering through the speeches, we applauded the final speaker and headed for the Casino. Katherine was as anxious as I was reluctant to see it. Determined to get it over with as quickly as possible, I squelched my thoughts of the past as I guided her through the various gambling rooms and on to the Salon Rose with its risqué ceiling mural. The mini tour was completed on the terrace with its splendid view of the cliffs and the sea.

"Breathtaking," I sighed as I took in the panoramic view. I couldn't help being awed by its beauty.

"Absolutely breathtaking," a voice behind me reiterated. My heart skipped a beat. My lips quivered. I would know that deep rich voice anywhere. I knew I had to face him, but I held off for a long moment, trying to gain some composure. Then I swirled around to confront him.

"You look devastatingly beautiful, Olivia," Rick said smoothly.

Ignoring his remark, I said the first thing that entered my mind, "What are you doing here?"

"The same as you, I imagine. I was invited by Liberty United Bank to support research for breast cancer."

As he spoke, his chiseled jaw-line was firm, but his eyes were soft and gentle. They left me weak-kneed and crumbling. I had to get out of there. "Yes, of course. You'll have to excuse me. I was just leaving," I said as I looked beyond him and took a step to bypass him.

Rick stepped sideways to block me. "Walk with me in the gardens before you leave. Please, Olivia, that's all I ask."

I met his eyes levelly and, after quick consideration, nodded. It was time we had this out. He guided me out to the gardens with his hand at my waist, in itself unsettling.

We walked slowly along the garden path as Rick began, "First, let me tell you how sorry I am about Angie."

He had struck a cord and I stiffened.

"Flowers and cards were not enough. I should have been there for you. At the time, I was afraid I would just make things worse if I showed up after all the time that had passed, but now I think I was wrong to stay away. I should have gone to you, and let you decide if you wanted me there or not. I know what she meant to you. You have been so strong, so amazing through it all."

I looked at him questioningly, wondering how he could judge if I were strong or not.

Reading the look on my face, he answered, "Oh, I've watched you from afar. I've followed your career, read your books."

Fine, I thought, pin a medal on you, but I said nothing.

"Now I want to apologize for what happened in the Casino the last time we were here." He paused and gestured toward a bench. When we were seated, he took a deep breath and went on. "Olivia, my gambling started in college. It seemed harmless enough, a bet on a game now and then. I got lucky and won a sizeable sum of money. It seemed like an easy way to make a few bucks. One thing led to another and before I knew it, I was hooked. I'd bet on anything, just for the high it gave me. To make a long story short, once I realized my gambling was out of control, I stopped. That was it, and I never gambled again until we were here in the Casino. I should have told you about my problem, but I honestly thought I could handle it. I didn't want to bring you to Monaco and then deprive you of seeing the legendary Monte Carlo Casino, but the main reason I didn't say anything was because I was ashamed to tell you that gambling had once had a grip on me.

"As soon as I returned home, I joined Gamblers Anonymous. From them, I learned that gambling is an ongoing addiction. It's like a disease that can't be cured, only controlled. I have never gambled again since that horrible night. I had every intention of coming back to you, of fighting for you, of doing whatever it took to bring us back together, until I realized that it would be like asking you to accept me with an incurable illness. It would be unfair to ask that of you. I've got it under control, but there are no guarantees. That's why I didn't call you or try to see you.

"For a year or so, I couldn't even look at another woman. I focused on work, for lack of anything else in my life. It didn't help ease the pain or dull the memories, so, desperate for relief, I tried another approach. I went after anything in a skirt, sometimes juggling three or four women at a time. I found that I was even more miserable, because I compared every woman I met to you, and they always fell short. There was no comparison.

"Then, somewhere along the line, I met Tiffany."

My face registered knowledge of his failed marriage.

He went on. "I went for her for all the wrong reasons. I knew it would be safe, because I didn't love her. That's terrible, I know, but I had vowed never to fall in love again. She seemed satisfied with what I could give her, until we were married. Things went from bad to worse, until finally, I ended it. I tried to make it up to her with a generous settlement. She's remarried now, and happier than ever.

"When I saw you that day at the Four Seasons, I realized that I would never be over you. And your proper greeting, but obvious avoidance of me, gave me hope that you had not gotten over me. If you could have smiled warmly and looked me straight in the eye without holding back, I would have given up, packed it in. But you couldn't.

It wasn't much to go on, but I knew afterward that I had to try. That's when I set up our little run-in at the park."

My eyes widened in astonishment, and I opened my mouth to protest, but Rick quickly continued. "I know it was a bad idea, but I'm not sorry for trying. I'm just sorry that it didn't work. And I found out from that meeting that you're engaged. So, as badly as it went, at least it did serve a purpose."

"And now you're taking advantage of this situation." It was a statement, not a question.

"Olivia, I'm doing what I should have done five years ago. I should have come after you, explained the reasons for my behavior. That doesn't make it right, I know, but maybe understanding the circumstances and my history, you might be able to forgive me. I can't change the past, but I can fight for the future. One thing I know for sure. What we have is rare. It can't be replaced. Do I deserve another chance? Probably not, but our love does."

While Rick spoke my mood had graduated from nervous to skeptical to irritated. Now I was angry. "So now, after all that's happened, now that you've decided you're good and ready, I'm supposed to drop everything, end my engagement, and pick up right where we left off. Have I got that straight?"

For the first time, Rick's lips curved in a hint of a smile. He had always enjoyed getting me fired up, but realizing that now was not the time, he caught himself. He moved lithely from the bench to the ground before me onto one knee. As he reached for my hand, I pulled away, but he held on firmly, squeezing it tightly in his. "To be honest, Livie, that's exactly what I would like to have happen, but I know I can't expect that. I can't tell you what you should do or feel, but I'm asking you to forgive me."

"Please don't do this, Rick."

"I can't live with it anymore. I have no choice. Can you forgive me?"

My religious upbringing kicked in. How could I withhold forgiveness from someone so repentant? "Yes, I forgive you. It was a long time ago. Everyone makes mistakes. I've moved on, and so should you."

"Thank you," he said as he pressed his lips to my hand, kissing it gently. "You don't know what this means to me."

Uncomfortable and agitated, I jerked my hand harshly from his grasp and stood up. "I have to get back," I said sharply.

We walked back to the Casino silently until we reached the doors. Before opening the door, Rick leaned toward me, our eyes just inches apart, and whispered, "This is not over. I love you, Olivia, and I'm going to fight for you."

I could only stare at the steely determination in his eyes.

Delivering me to the group of writers gathered at the bar, Katherine among them, Rick gave me one last glance, and with a confident smile and a wicked wink, he left.

"I wondered where you'd disappeared to. Who was that handsome specimen?" Katherine nosed.

"Just an old friend," I answered casually.

"I don't have any 'old friends' that look like that," she said accusingly.

"How unfortunate," I responded lightly. I couldn't help it. The woman annoyed me and was just looking to cause trouble. I was glad we were leaving tomorrow and I would be rid of her.

Chapter Fourteen

On the long flight home, I closed my eyes to avoid conversation with Katherine and to review in my mind the events of the previous night. I had to admit I was touched by Rick's openness about his gambling after all this time, as well as his sincerity in seeking my forgiveness. I still knew him well enough to know that it was no act. I had been wrong in believing that he had purposely set me up, that he had targeted me as part of a grand scheme to con me out of money. Perhaps I too needed forgiving.

I smiled inwardly at the thought of his parting words. Like bells, they chimed in my head, "This is not over. I love you, Olivia, and I'm going to fight for you." What would he do, I wondered, before I caught myself and shook the thought from my mind.

Trey was happy to hear from me when I called him from my apartment, and as he picked up on my carefree mood during dinner, he seemed to relax and the furrow between his brows gradually disappeared. Out of his inborn respect for privacy, he never asked me point blank if I had dealt with whatever had been bothering me. He took the return of my happy disposition as answer enough that all was well.

The only blip on our radar was our disagreement about setting a date for the wedding. Trey was pushing to set the date. He favored late summer or early fall. I wasn't ready to be pinned down to a date, especially one so soon. I was in the throes of wrapping up my third novel, and I didn't want to rush my work or the plans for the wedding. Trey said he understood, but was still keeping the pressure on.

I, myself, didn't quite understand the reason for my new lease on life. The issues with Rick remained unresolved, but in spite of that, or was it because of it, the cloud of discontentment had lifted.

I arrived at the office early Monday morning and was busy sifting through mail and memos when I looked up to find Trey standing in the doorway. "Good morning, Sweetheart. Come in. Just put that stuff on the floor," I said, waving at the stack of reference books piled on the chair.

Oddly, he didn't move, but stayed planted in the doorway, feet apart, hands at his sides.

"Or not," I said, making a face at his unresponsive pose.

"Katherine popped into my office last night to tell me all about her trip," he said with a surly attitude. He paused as though he had asked a question.

Observing him more carefully, I saw that Trey's face was ashen. His eyes were steely and cold, and his body rigid. Suddenly, I realized what this was about. "And . . ." I said, waiting.

"And she told me that on the night of the gala you met up with a man and left with him, only to return much later. She described him as young and exotically good-looking, among other things."

"Well, if Katherine said it, then it must be true," I hissed.

"Is it? Is it true?" His piercing blue eyes were cold and accusing.

Obviously Katherine had purposely left plenty of room for implication and innuendo in her version of what had occurred that night. I was furious that she had pulled this stunt to drive a wedge between Trey and me, but I would deal with her later. Right now, I was outraged that Trey would for a moment think the worst of me based on her unsubstantiated story.

I decided to let him burn in his own flames. "As a matter of fact, yes, it is true," I stated calmly, and I picked up my pencil, lowered my head, and said quietly, "Now, if you'll excuse me, I have work to do."

"Olivia, it was Rick, wasn't it?" he challenged angrily. Trey was aware of the depth of my previous relationship with Rick from the intimate disclosures in *Journey of Love.*

I'd had enough. The Italian blood in me took over. Leaping from my chair, I leaned across the desk, arms flailing, and shouted, "Why ask me? Why not ask Katherine? You seem to believe everything she said or implied, so why bother asking me now?"

"Because I want to know the truth!" he scowled.

"Right, I can see you're ready to listen to the truth!" I spit out sarcastically. I grabbed my purse and started for the door where Trey stood blocking my way. Seething, I glared up at him, "In case you hadn't noticed, this is neither the time nor the place. Now get out of my way."

He had never seen me this angry. Unwilling to push me any further, he stepped aside, and I strode past him and down the hall to the steps. I was in no mood to wait for an elevator.

I rushed from the building that housed the offices of Horizon House Publishing full of frustration and anger. Relief was nowhere in sight until I found myself on Fifth Avenue, paradise of a woman scorned. So, naturally, I decided to console myself with an impromptu shopping spree. I traipsed in and out of stores, picking and choosing, spending a great deal of money on things I didn't need - perfume, lace handkerchiefs, ridiculously priced shoes, and a hat that I knew I would never wear. But there was still no relief.

Then, in desperation, I did what every red-blooded woman does when she has man troubles; I ate. Comfort foods get their name honestly, I figured, so I drowned my sorrows in hot fudge, not to mention maple syrup, gravy, and cheese sauce. It didn't help the problem, except by way of diversion when I got on the scale. By then, though, my anger had mellowed to confusion.

It had now been three days since the argument. Trey had called me repeatedly at home and on my cell phone, leaving messages that we needed to talk, but I didn't feel like talking. I wasn't ready to talk. I didn't know yet what to say. Finally, I had left him a message saying that I needed some time, to please stop calling, and that I would get back to him when I was ready.

Since then, the silence had been deafening. I checked my messages compulsively and when there were none I was both relieved and disappointed.

I had never seen Trey so angry or so hurt as he was that morning. His anger had, in turn, infuriated me. How could he give credence to Katherine's story without asking me first? He had judged me before giving me a chance to defend myself. I didn't need defending, I told myself, only a chance to explain. The fact that Trey hadn't given me the benefit of the doubt bothered me, seriously bothered me. The unmistakable hurt that he had masked with coldness bothered me too. I hated seeing him hurting, and felt guilty for causing him pain, but he brought it on himself, didn't he? If he had come to me before assuming the worst, it could have been avoided. My emotions continued to vacillate between anger and guilt.

Why hadn't I told him that I had seen Rick? Was it because he wouldn't understand, because it would have hurt him, or because I felt guilty? Trey wasn't a hothead or some macho type who wouldn't understand. Was I afraid that he would understand only too well? Rick had wanted to explain and be forgiven, so that he would finally have closure, I told myself. But what about his parting words, "This is not over . . .?" Not the words of someone seeking closure. I didn't know any more. The harder I tried to sort things out, the more scrambled it all became.

I decided to take a break and go home to Laurel and my family and friends. I cleared some time on my calendar and notified the office.

As the cab drove off, I looked at the house I had grown up in. From the dormers on the Cape Cod roof to the little front porch, it was home. Inside, everything was just as I had left it, except for the fresh arrangement of tulips and daffodils on the kitchen table, which the cleaning lady had picked and arranged for my arrival. I left my suitcase and purse in the kitchen, and wandered aimlessly from room to room hearing the echo of laughter that had once filled the air.

An overwhelming melancholy enveloped me, until I entered Angie's room. She had chosen bright blue and white chintz for the bed and windows. I smiled at the Teddy Bear comfortably poised against the pillows on the bed. The dresser and chest of drawers were laden with pictures of our parents, of us as children, and many photos of me, the most recent the picture from my first book jacket. The copy of *Journey of Love* that I had given her rested on the night stand next to the bed. I opened it to the inscription I had written:

To my loving sister Angie,
to whom I owe everything
and without whom this book
would not have been possible.
We did it!--

All my love,
Livie

The pressure of the tears I had held back for so long was more than I could handle. They poured out uncontrollably, and I cried long and hard until I could cry no more. Like popping the cork of vintage champagne, once the pressure had been released all was mellow and good, and I wondered why I had held it in for such a long time. That night I slept soundly in my old bed.

Over the next few days, I visited with my aunt and uncle, cousins and friends. It felt surprisingly good to be back, to catch up on news and the latest gossip, putter in the yard, drive to the drugstore, and relax.

I called Roy and we met for lunch one afternoon. As we sat across from each other, I took pride in his striking good looks. His skin was tanned, and his chest and shoulders broad from working outdoors with his construction company. The fine head of curly hair, streaked golden by the sun, rested like a halo above his bronzed face, but his lively blue eyes confirmed that there was no mistaking him for an angel. Roy was sexy, no doubt about it. His looks were enough to get any woman's attention, but what really won their hearts was the openness and warmth of his personality. And his trademark sense of humor. Seeing him again took me back to when we first met.

My girlfriend and I frequented a local nightspot, Let's Dance, at least once a week, presumably to do just that - dance. And if we just happened to meet Mr. Right along the way, so be it. One night we were out for a night of fun and the possibility of romance. It was late. We had met up with a few friends and had been dancing for hours, as a group, in a large circle monopolizing the dance floor. The top forties-type band was loud and still going full force.

"I need a break," I gasped to Deb.

"And a drink," she agreed, as she followed me off the dance floor.

We pressed between bodies lining the bar three deep.

"What can I get you ladies?" the bartender yelled over the music.

"Two vodka and tonics, please."

We were awaiting our drinks and doing emergency repair work on our hair and makeup when, from somewhere close behind me, I heard, "Howdy, Ma'am."

I turned around to face the owner of the voice and found this tall hunk standing before me grinning from ear to ear and wearing the biggest cowboy hat I had ever seen. It was made of startlingly bright aqua foam rubber and rose about two feet into the air with a brim span of almost a yard. At a fair in Texas, it might be acceptable, but this was Ohio, not Texas, and definitely not a country western kind of place.

"Care to dance, Ma'am?" he asked, touching the brim of the ridiculous hat, the broad smile still covering his ruggedly handsome face.

I was sure that I was the butt of a private joke, but he was so good-looking and his eyes seemed too kind to be cruel. I decided to take a chance. So what if I was seen dancing with the only giant cowboy hat in the state. He was too cute to throw back. "Only if you promise not to call me Ma'am ever again," I warned.

We danced to several songs while others gawked, and then found a table where we sat and talked as we nursed our drinks.

Finally, he removed the enormous hat and let me in on the joke. He had told his buddy that any girl who would agree to dance with him while he wore that outlandish hat would surely be confident and have a good sense of humor, qualities he was apparently looking for in a woman. He had wondered around the club, carefully stalking his prey. I was the third one he had approached. The other two had laughed in his face and turned tail.

I wasn't sure if that made me confident or pathetic.

At twenty-seven, my goal in life was to be married. I was feeling the tick tock of my biological clock. The thought of being alone forever scared me to death. I wanted the husband, the two point five kids, the dog, and the picket fence. Roy was everything that I was not - outgoing, aggressive, life-of-the-party, and strong-willed. He was a leader and I was happy to be his follower.

We were married less than a year later.

The first few months of marriage turned out to be easier than I expected. I anticipated a rough adjustment period during which both parties vie for control and try to find their place in their new roles as husband and wife. That's what I had read anyway. But we didn't seem to fall into that pattern, and I took it as a good sign. Our marriage would not have to endure the pitfalls many others suffered. We were just two people in love. It came easily.

Until we hit the wall. It happened about a year later. It was just as abrupt and painful as physically running into a brick wall, and as impossible to ignore.

I attended a weeklong tax seminar in Columbus, about two hours away from our home. I needed the continuing education credits, and it didn't hurt to get an update on the latest changes in tax laws. My employer agreed to pay for half of the cost, so it was a fairly good deal. At any rate, it was necessary for my accounting career and when I explained the situation to Roy he seemed fine with it. I called him throughout the week while I was gone, having to leave messages most of the time. He called me back at least twice.

The seminar ended Friday around three o'clock. I put the pedal to the metal whenever traffic allowed. I was so anxious to get home and into my handsome husband's arms. As I drove, I pictured the scene of my arrival in my mind. I'll bet he has a surprise waiting for me. Maybe he's taking me to my favorite restaurant. Better yet, he's cooked a special dinner for us so we can stay in, get cozy, catch up on details, and make love, not necessarily in that order. I wonder if he bought me roses, my favorite flowers, to welcome me home. No, the flowers are too much. Even my romantic mind knows when it's wandered too far from reality.

I zipped the car up the drive and jumped out dragging my suitcase full of a week's worth of dirty clothes behind me. I knocked on the door with my knuckles as I balanced purse, books, and suitcase. No answer. I fumbled to free a hand to turn the doorknob. Everything started slipping and before I could catch them, books, purse and contents, and suitcase clattered to the ground around me. Still no sign of life. "Roy! Roy, I'm home!" No answer. His car was in the garage. He had to be home. He must be hiding till I find the surprise.

I retrieved all that had fallen and headed for the kitchen. Relieving myself of the case, I deposited my books and purse on the table, which, instead of being set for an intimate dinner, was heaped with newspapers, magazines, and unopened mail. The smell of something gaseous and rather foul seeped from a pot on the stove. "Roy, I'm home," I called again. Still no answer. I walked down the hall, turned the corner into the living room, and stopped short.

Roy was slouched on the couch in torn T-shirt and paint-stained cutoffs, with a week's growth on his face. Dirty dishes, beer cans, and debris of all sorts littered the tabletops and floor. Not the picture I had dreamed of coming home to. But the awful, really ugly part of it was that he was pretending to be asleep.

Why would anyone think they could get away with faking sleep? Or is that the point – to let you know they're faking it? At any rate, it was as plain as the nose on his face - Roy was faking it.

It seems like such a small thing, but after that, things were never the same between Roy and me. I couldn't explain it then, and I still can't, but from that moment on, we were no longer close. We no longer shared secrets. The trust was gone. We very seldom were intimate. When we did make love, it was out of a sense of duty or physical need, lacking the tenderness and joy of pleasing each other. I don't know what happened during the time I was gone, and I probably never will, but it changed everything.

We had hit the wall. There was no denying or escaping it. No going back. No matter how much we wished we could.

Even after the divorce papers were signed, sealed, and delivered, we both wanted to try to patch things up. For almost a year, we tried to reconcile, going to counseling, reading self-help books, attending a marriage retreat, until we had to accept that the light had gone out of our marriage, and that maybe we were just meant to be good friends.

And we are, to this day, the best of friends. And we do still love each other, just not as husband and wife.

"You're new career must agree with you," he said approvingly, startling me back to the present. "I've never seen you look better. I mean you've always been a knockout, but your dark eyes and delicate features seem even more outstanding now."

My face flushed at the uncharacteristic compliment. "Thanks, it must be the running," I said timidly.

After the usual small talk, he filled me in on his latest conquests. It was odd that it didn't bother me when he spoke of his relationships with women. Amazed that my feelings could change so much, I wondered what it took to make love stick.

"So I hear you're engaged to that big shot publisher," Roy said, with more than a little negativity. He had met Trey only briefly at Angie's funeral. It always astonished me how men could take so little of what they dished out.

"Yes, I am," I said briefly, in consideration of his sizable male ego.

"Just because he's an executive in New York doesn't mean you have to take anything from him, you know."

"Roy, I think you know me better than that."

"True. It's just that you deserve the best," he said sheepishly, "and I don't want anybody shortchanging you."

"Thank you. I appreciate that," I said softly.

"He's not American, is he?"

"No, he's British," I answered, having a good idea where this was going.

"You have to watch those limeys. Never know what they're liable to do."

Understanding that this was Roy's way of showing his concern for me, I reached over and patted his hand reassuringly, "Don't worry, I will."

I had slept in one morning until almost ten and was in the kitchen preparing my first caffeine hit of the day when the doorbell rang. It was Saturday and I wasn't expecting anyone. I peeked out the window, but could only see a car in the drive. It took me a minute to realize where I had seen that car before. It can't be, I gasped, as I quickly ran my fingers through my hair and smoothed my T-shirt and capris on my way to the door. When I opened it, I couldn't believe my eyes.

There stood Rick, casually dressed in shorts and holding a tennis racket. "You ready?" he asked nonchalantly, as if in a time warp and the last five years had never happened.

I stood in the doorway, dumbfounded.

"We'd better get a move on if we want to get a court," he said and smiled widely. "May I come in?" he asked, taking my arm and leading me back into the foyer.

"How did you know I was here?" I stammered, still not believing my eyes.

"I called your office. They said you had business to attend to at home for a few days."

"They're not supposed to give out that information."

"Well, you know how persuasive I can be."

"Don't I though," I said arching my eyebrows, but I ended up breaking into a smile. I couldn't get over the fact that he had followed me home, and for the moment at least, I had to admit I was glad to see him.

"Now get your racket. We're wasting good sunshine."

It was a warm, cloudless day. He had kept his red convertible, and riding in the sun with the wind against my skin I forgot all that had happened since my last ride in Rick's Mustang.

After six grueling sets of tennis, we stopped for lunch at the A&W Root Beer stand, taking advantage of the curbside service. "I haven't eaten in a car in years," I laughed.

"For you, only the best," he answered with a wink.

When we had downed our hot dogs and frosted mugs of root beer, the conversation turned serious as we reminisced about Angie. We got back on the road, but I noticed we weren't headed for the neighborhood. "This isn't the way home," I remarked.

"No, but it's somewhere I think you need to go," Rick said, placing his hand over mine.

He made a quick stop at a nearby florist's and a few minutes later we turned into the cemetery. The grass was freshly mowed and the heady smell, mixed with the scent of flowers left by loved ones, floated in the air like nature's incense. Surprisingly, Rick knew right where Angie's grave lay. We walked to it together and arranged the flowers in the in-ground vase. He held my hand and steadied me as I spoke silently to my sister. Before we left, he also bowed his head in prayer.

On the way home, I turned to him, "Thank you. I hadn't been able to do it alone."

"I know," he said, squeezing my hand.

Rick made it impossible to say no to dinner with him that night. I donned a floral skirt with matching sweater set in pale pink, and my mother's pearls at my neck.

I left it to him to decide on the restaurant, expecting him to choose the only four-star restaurant in Laurel. Instead, he pulled into the parking lot of Angelo's, a quaint little Italian eatery famous for their "homemade" sauce. I couldn't have been more pleased. The atmosphere was typical with red and white checked tablecloths, Chianti bottles lit with candles, and "O Sole Mio" playing in the background. It had a cozy and comfortable charm.

Seated at a table by the window, we perused the menu. Rick ordered his favorite, a hearty Cabernet Sauvignon, and I chose a lighter rosé to go with our orders of pasta. When our drinks arrived, he toasted, "As Dorothy so aptly put it, 'There's no place like home.'"

Holding my glass to his, I agreed, "No place like home," and drank deeply. I was suddenly nervous that I was there sitting across from Rick. What was I doing? The entire day had been one surprise after another. I wasn't prepared for this. I had come home to think, and hopefully untangle my feelings for Trey, to get back on track, but instead I was here with Rick.

And what was this all about anyway? It had been over between us for a long time. He had his life, and I, mine. It was okay, I guess, to talk about the good old days and to show compassion for a friend. I supposed that's what we were now, friends once again. So why was I uncomfortable? Would I feel guilty later? The last thing I needed was another burden of guilt to shoulder.

Lost in my thoughts, I had forgotten how Rick could read my mind. It was uncanny, really. No wonder he was so successful in business; knowing what the other party was thinking certainly made it easier to negotiate. His sensitivity, I knew, stemmed from the prejudice he had faced growing up in a conservative suburban community. His parents had been the only Asian and white couple in Laurel. They were respected members of the community now, but when they had first moved in, there had been a lot of talk and several incidents. Rick had explained to me that, as the oldest of his brothers and sister, he had to pave the way in school, defending himself and them without being labeled a troublemaker. As a means of self-preservation, he had learned quickly how to read people. The lesson had served him well.

"Liv? Livie?" His deep chocolate voice brought me out of my reverie. "It's just dinner. We both have to eat, don't we?" he cajoled.

"Yes, I guess so," I said, unsure of what to do.

"Let's just relax and enjoy our meal before it gets cold. No need to worry. I won't bite. Not tonight, anyway," he said with a wicked grin.

The rich aroma of tomato sauce reminded me how hungry I was. I yielded, my concern put to rest for the time being. "If this tastes as good as it smells, I may never leave."

Dinner went on smoothly from there. We ate and drank and traded quips of the past.

"Remember when we first met?" Rick said. "You dumped all your pens and pencils on the floor, you were so nervous."

"How could I forget?"

"Your face turned as red as . . . as this tomato sauce, but something about those dark olive eyes rendered me helpless, and I knew right then that I was hooked."

"It was probably just hunger, what with tomato sauce and olives and all," I joked.

"No, because I knew for sure the next time we met, when you ran smack into me as I opened the door to the stairs. The heat of your body and the scent of you drove me crazy."

"But as I remember, you barely skipped a beat."

"Fast reaction time, but believe me, I was reeling inside."

Guiding the conversation away from the personal, I brought up Rick's career. "You've been very successful since those days at Leonard Kistler."

"Yes, I've been fortunate. My management consulting firm has grown beyond my expectations. Griffith and Sloane, Inc. is now Sloane Enterprises. I bought out my partner, Ted Griffith, about a year ago. But what about you? You changed careers, became a successful writer, and never looked back."

"Yes, well, things just sort of fell into place," I said, not wanting to get into the reason I started writing.

"I've read your books. They're thought provoking. They reflect you, your romantic nature, and your values. I felt closer to you when I read them."

I was at a loss for words. "Thank you," was all I could say.

In the car on the way home, Rick reached for my hand and held it firmly. A pulse flickered from him to me until I pulled my hand away, ostensibly to search for my keys. He walked me to the front door, and after unlocking it, I turned to thank him for a lovely evening. As he stepped toward me, I withdrew until my back was against the house. With one hand on the house, he leaned close as he placed the other under my chin, tilting my face to him. Our lips were barely an inch apart. A glittering heat swept over me and shamelessly flared in my eyes as his flashed his own smoldering burn. "I'll call you in New York," he said softly, his tone belying the tight set of his jaw. Then he turned and left as abruptly as he had arrived that morning, the taillights of the red Mustang disappearing in the darkness.

I slumped against the house, breathless, letting the heat within me, the heat he had caused, slowly evaporate into the cool night air.

Chapter Fifteen

I called Trey the morning I returned to New York. To his credit, he had not called or left any further messages, which made me all the more anxious to talk to him. When he spoke, instead of the relief I expected to hear in his voice, I was startled by the indifference in his tone. If it was a ploy to scare me, it was working. I asked him to meet me that night at the Bull and Bear, the bar in the Waldorf Astoria. It was small and quiet, good for conversation. Now if only I knew what to say.

We arrived simultaneously and took seats in the leopard-covered chairs, the safari decor transporting us into the jungles of Africa.

Getting our drink orders out of the way, Trey spoke first, "How are you, Olivia? You look wonderful, as always." His voice was bland, and his eyes, usually sparkling and bright, were hooded and a dull gray.

"I'm . . . well . . . to be honest, I'm confused," I blurted, searching for a chink in his armor and disappointed to find none.

He took a long swallow of the Glenlivet that had just arrived. "How can *I* help?" he sighed, sounding certain that he couldn't.

Dreading a scene similar to the one that took place in the office, I asked hesitantly, "Trey, why did you think the worst of me before giving me a chance to explain?"

"Because you hid the fact that you met your ex-lover there. You kept that from me for a reason. Guilt is the obvious reason." Trey said it in a matter-of-fact, almost uninterested tone.

"Nothing like jumping to conclusions!" My voice rose two octaves. "I didn't hide anything. There was nothing to hide. I didn't meet Rick there, as in a planned meeting. I ran into him. There were three hundred guests. He happened to be one of them. I guess I should have considered the possibility that he would be there, but Matt Jennings told me, when I subtly inquired, that Rick had business dealings in Chicago that would require his attention. After that, I never gave it another thought. *My* mistake," I sneered.

I took a breath and calmed myself before going on, carefully lowering my voice. "Rick took me aside to ask for my forgiveness. You know what happened between us back about what seems like a lifetime ago. That's all he wanted, forgiveness." I was leaving out the "This is not over" part, but I could only fix one thing at a time, and besides, it seemed irrelevant now. "I admit I was on edge about going to Monte Carlo. I feared the memories, but then I decided it would be good for me to confront those fears once and for all, so that you and I could have a fresh start on our life together." I stopped, out of breath and out of steam.

Trey's complexion had gone gray, but his eyes brightened. "I know how much you loved him. When I heard you had seen him, well, all my insecurities took over. I know we don't have what..."

"Stop!" I ordered, holding my hand up. "Stop right there. I won't have you disclaiming what we have. No two relationships are alike. They can't be compared."

Trey seemed at a loss for words. "I'm sorry for doubting you, Olivia, truly sorry," and the tortured look on his face proved it.

"Please, don't say anything yet," I warned, "I have to tell you, Trey, I want to tell you," I rephrased, "that while I was home, I saw Rick again. I had no idea he would be there. There was a knock on the door one day and there he was." I saw Trey's eyes darken. "I spent the day with him, talking about old times, our careers, and most importantly, Angie. He took me to the cemetery. I think it was his way of making up for not being around when she died. It was comforting."

Trey's expression was far from happy, but he seemed accepting of this new information. "Where does that leave us?" he asked.

"I've tried my hardest to sort things out, but as I said at the beginning, I'm confused. Everything that's happened in the last five years has just now caught up with me. Before I can move forward confidently, I have to work through all the changes in my life. I need time, Trey, time and patience from you. I hope you can understand."

"I'm trying to understand, but I must admit it's difficult. I want you to be happy, Olivia. I want us to be happy together, so if it will help, I'll wait until you are ready. We can postpone any discussion of wedding plans. Is that fair enough?"

"Fair enough," I smiled, and he managed a warm, if weak, smile back.

We settled back into our comfortable routine and I hoped that the worst was over. I was in the rewrite stages of my third book. To no one's surprise, it wasn't going well. I had learned from experience that strong emotions inspire strong, powerful text; jumbled emotions lack inspiration entirely and make for a jumbled, incoherent piece of work. I had worked with Trey on my novels from the very beginning. He had always guided me to clarity and single-mindedness, but now he was part of the problem, instead of the solution. For the first time, working with him was becoming difficult.

In the conference room, seated around the long table, the seven of us met this Monday morning as usual. After everyone refilled their coffee mugs and grabbed for the last doughnut, Trey began the meeting by addressing the loose-ends left from the prior week. Then several staff members reported on the status of their work and the writers they represented. Eventually, the literary magazine became the topic of discussion. The deadline was fast approaching and several articles were reported to be almost complete, but there were still no ideas for the monthly column, where new ideas and styles of writing were discussed, explained, and critiqued. The room fell silent as everyone wracked their brains for an idea.

"How about this?" I chirped, and heads turned toward me, eager to hear a solution. "We do a column on lyricists. We pick several from different genres of music, say pop, show tunes, and rap. We compare their lyrics, the similarities, differences, and unique qualities. We do the same with the writers themselves, comparing their ages, life styles, backgrounds. What do you think?"

Many heads nodded approval. Eric, the young poet and newest member of the group, was the first to speak up. "I like it," he said enthusiastically, as his head buoyed like a bobble doll in the rear window of a car. "Comparing Sean P Ditty Comb's lyrics to, say, Paul McCartney's is bound to spark controversy."

Trey had a stodgy look on his face. "We're not music critics. This isn't one of those music rags they publish by the hundreds. It isn't what we do," he said dismissively.

"Well, maybe it should be," I said, defending my idea. At least I had an idea, I thought. "Artists and writers are usually the first to be open-minded and accepting of new and different styles and genres," I reminded him.

Without even acknowledging my response, Trey led the meeting to the next subject on the agenda, tabling any further discussion of the column. I sat back, trying to hide my frustration by plastering a look of placid indifference on my face, but inside, my blood was boiling. It was one thing to reject an idea, but it was another to dismiss the person who made the suggestion.

Trey knew how hard I had to fight to gain and keep the respect of the staff because of our personal relationship. I had overheard many a snide remark, and been the butt of many a joke since we had started dating. Instead of supporting me, or at the very least, respecting my opinion, he had humiliated me in front of everyone.

It didn't take a rocket scientist to see what was behind his behavior. He was getting even, in the only safe way he could, for the incidents with Rick and for putting our wedding plans on hold.

In the interest of avoiding another scene at work, I left the building as soon as the meeting adjourned. I changed into my running clothes and ran my regular route in Central Park, hoping to clear my head and jog some sense into it. Why was everything so difficult now, I wondered?

When I got home, I checked my messages. The shoes I had been waiting for were in. Rachael wanted to meet for lunch. Trey had called. His apology sounded more politically correct than sincere.

"That's strong," I complained to the answering machine, "humiliate me in public, and then apologize privately."

After his message, a voice came on low and smooth, "Olivia, I'm in New York on business for a few days. I'd like to have dinner with you. I'll call again later." It was amazing what just the sound of his voice could do. I felt fluttering in my stomach and a flush cover my face. I wouldn't go, of course, but I replayed the message three times before erasing it.

Tuesday I worked at home on the rewrite of a section of my novel. Trey said it needed revision, more characterization, but I liked it the way it was. After all, I wasn't creating caricatures of people, but real people.

Around five, the phone rang. Trey, I assumed, as I picked up the phone. "Hello?"

"This is a warning call. Dinner and I will be there in an hour, okay?" the deep voice said.

"Rick?"

"*Okay*?" he repeated.

"That sounds great, but . . ." and before I could qualify my answer I heard the dial tone.

Although annoyed by his audacity, I had no choice but to get ready. I rushed to shower and shampoo my hair. I shaved my legs and then questioned why I was bothering. I'm wearing pants anyway. Was it the possibility of them coming off that concerned me? No, no, don't be ridiculous, I told myself. I'm engaged. He's a charmer, for sure, but that won't be happening. Those days are over.

I threw on white jeans with a white blouse, rolled up the sleeves and slipped into my little sandals with crystal butterflies. A touch of sparkle never hurt. I finished off with a mist of Chanel No. 5, the only perfume that didn't make me sneeze.

I straightened the living room, plumping pillows and hiding old newspapers and magazines. Then I set the dining room table with Royal Dalton china and Waterford crystal, both my mother's. I was debating on the music when the doorbell rang. I quickly opted for smooth jazz as a safe pick before answering the door.

Rick stood tanned and solid in his jeans and Polo shirt. He held a large bag that was permeating the hallway with a mouth-watering aroma. "I hope you're hungry for Chinese tonight," he beamed.

"Mmmm, smells good."

From behind his back, he presented a bouquet of flowers, peach and cream roses, of course.

"Oh, my favorite. You remembered. They're lovely," I gushed, unable to help myself.

"So are you," Rick whispered as he kissed me on the cheek.

This is going to be a rough night, I sighed to myself, but I was determined to keep my guard up.

Inside, I started emptying the contents of the bag onto the kitchen counter. He had brought a veritable buffet of Chinese dishes. "Looks like you bought out the place."

"I couldn't make up my mind."

"There's a lot of that going around," I mumbled softly.

"What's that?"

"Nothing," I spoke up, making a mental note to be more careful.

"No, no, no," he said when he saw me emptying the little white boxes into bowls.

"What?"

"Do you have a blanket?"

"Of course, but..."

"Would you get it, please? I'm setting the table tonight. The dining room looks great, but not for tonight."

I could see that he was going to make this very difficult. He spread the blanket on the living room floor and placed all the little white cartons on it. Then, he transferred the place settings of china, silver, and crystal onto the blanket. Equipped with his own music, he loaded the CD's, beginning with Respighi's Ancient Air and Dances. "Now we're ready to eat," he announced and stopped, thinking of something, and added "almost." After another trip to the dining room, Rick returned with the roses, which I had arranged in a vase. Placing the flowers in the center of the blanket, he took inventory and declared, "Now we can eat."

Although I knew he had his own agenda, whatever it might be, I couldn't help but think it was sweet of him to go to so much trouble, and to remember that some of our happiest times were laughing and talking and eating on the floor in the living room.

My earlier annoyance melted away as I relaxed and enjoyed the impromptu picnic. Always amusing and insightful, Rick enthralled me with his views on everything from politics to the current ladies fashions. He kept the mood light and fun.

Before I knew it, the evening was over and he was gone. I folded the blanket, with taunting thoughts of his strong shoulders, the firmness of his body, his satiny gold skin, those self-assured hands. He had been a perfect gentleman. I would have rebuffed any advances, but I was ashamed to admit I was disappointed that I hadn't had to.

Chapter Sixteen

The following day, our usual Wednesday meeting was canceled because Trey had to make a trip to the Chicago office. I was glad. I had decided not to make an issue of the staff meeting incident, but the more time I had to cool down, the better. He would be back late Friday and we were going to dinner and the theater Saturday night.

I caught myself daydreaming in front of the computer more than once since last night's dinner with Rick. The roses on my desk definitely were not helping my concentration. I removed them to my bedroom. Not good either, I decided. They looked perfect on the coffee table in the living room, but then I pictured our dinner on the blanket, and that was out. Finally, they were banished to the kitchen.

I tried to picture Trey eating dinner on a blanket on the living room floor. I couldn't. That's not fair, I told myself. It's just not his style. He's English and proper and refined. There's nothing wrong with that.

The two men were different as night and day, exact opposites, come to think of it. One was far younger than I, the other much older. One was dark, bold, and intense. The other was fair, cautious, and soft-spoken. One grew up in middle-class America. The other was raised in a grand manor in England. One shared his feelings openly. The other was naturally reserved. One was risky, the other safe. The decision should be easy, given their vast differences. I realized that they were not the problem. I was. I didn't know what I wanted.

Rick was smooth and charming and fun. I liked the way he made me feel when I was with him. He worked hard and played hard. He was smart and successful. I had loved him like no other. But he had hurt me more than I thought possible.

Trey was no slouch either. He could have had everything handed to him - money, land, title - but he had chosen to earn his own way. His career and reputation were built on merit. Trey had stood by me. He had shown me at times, when it counted, that his feelings ran deep. He was good, loyal, reliable, and faithful. I'm making him sound like a dog, I thought, disgusted with myself. I gave up my mental bantering and got back to work.

On Saturday I decided I deserved, and needed, a beauty day. I called Rachael, inviting her to join me. Her marriage to the butcher wasn't quite living up to her expectations. Odd, how we can start out hanging on someone's every word and a year or two later find them dull and lackluster. I had the impression that George's appeal may have had more to do with his bank account than his personality. Now that the financial crisis was over, so was Rachael's enthusiasm for the marriage. At any rate, she had the day free and said that she could use "all the help she could get" when it came to beauty, but the idea of a massage bothered her. She had never had one and was apprehensive of having a stranger's hands on her. "He better not try anything, or he won't be walking upright for a week."

"You can request a woman masseuse if that would make you more comfortable," I suggested.

"Yeah right, like I want some woman's hands all over me."

"It'll be fine," I assured her. "Trust me."

"If I had a dollar for every time I've heard that."

I scheduled our appointments and met her at the spa at one o'clock.

As we changed into thick white terrycloth robes, Rachael refused to remove her underwear, "I'm not walking around here without my undies," she declared.

"You don't have to. You'll be covered with a sheet, but you can leave them on if you like."

"I like," she said, wrapping the robe tighter around her.

I had requested that we be in the same room, hoping to ease Rachael's fears. We shuffled to the massage room in our robes and flip flops, and got situated on the tables under our sheets. Then our masseurs, Paolo and Dirk (they swore those were their real names) arrived. After Rachael warned Paolo to "Watch it" and snapped one "Hey, that hurt," I heard only soft moans and groans of pleasure before I became lost in my own relaxing trance.

When our time was up and the guys were leaving, Rachael asked Paolo for his card and his work schedule. I smiled. "Told you," I gloated.

"Yeah, you should have told me sooner."

I threw my hands in the air. "I give up."

We left the spa three hours later - polished, trimmed, sloughed, and waxed. If we didn't look beautiful, we certainly felt it. Rachael hugged me goodbye, an unusual gesture for her, and I caught a cab back to the apartment to get dressed for the evening.

I chose a black sheath with matching jacket. The jacket, short and embossed with red flowers around the bottom, would come in handy in the chilly September evening. At the last minute, I plucked my amethyst ring from my jewelry box and slipped it on my right hand, wondering idly what Rick was doing tonight.

Trey arrived, punctual as always. He was usually complimentary, but tonight his only comment was, "Great, you're ready," and scooted us off to dinner. All through dinner he seemed preoccupied, losing his train of thought several times. I had barely taken my last bite when he flagged the waiter for the check and rushed us to the theater.

Afterward, I suggested we stop at a little bistro, a favorite of ours, for a cocktail. Something was definitely wrong. I had to get to the bottom of it. I ordered a Cosmo, mostly because it was pink and drinking out of a martini glass gave me a feeling of sophistication. Trey drank Glenlivet instead of his usual after-dinner brandy.

"Okay, what's going on?" I could wait no longer.

"You wanted to stop for a drink," he said without looking me in the eye, and I realized he had been avoiding eye contact all night.

"Something's on your mind. You're not yourself tonight. What is it Trey?" I reached for his hand. "Please tell me."

He could hold back no longer. The words gushed out, flooding me with fear. "Olivia, it's no use. It won't work between us."

I opened my mouth to object, but he went on feverishly. "We've tried. You've tried. I know how hard you've tried to make this work, but love cannot be forced. I know that you think well of me, that you respect me, that you care for me. We both know that's not enough. You just don't feel that spark when you see me. I want a woman who is passionate about me, a woman whose toes curl when I kiss her. You'd be selling yourself short, and in the end, we'd both suffer for it. I love you, Livie. I have since the first day we met and had that silly interview, but I have to let you go." He held my hand tighter.

I had gone cold. My breath caught in my chest. My eyes were big as saucers and brimming with tears.

"This is not easy for me." His voice was unsteady now and, clearing his tightening throat, he paused as if to gather strength. "We need to face the reality that this is not going to work. You've tormented yourself too long, and in doing so, tormented me. We have to accept that it wasn't meant to be. It's an injustice to both of us to go on this way."

The misery and sadness had surfaced leaving his face sagging and hollow. It made my heart ache. At that moment, I thought him the bravest man that ever lived. I knew how painful this was for him, but nonetheless, he had taken the high road and had done what he thought best for both of us.

"I do love you," I cried as tears dripped from my face.

"Yes, I know, but not the way a wife loves a husband."

I couldn't let go. "It's just the timing. If I had more time . . ."

"We both know that's not true. We've been hiding behind it too long, skirting the real issue. Let's face facts. It's not there for you, Olivia. Stop fighting it. Do you think I haven't noticed that your eyes don't light up when I enter the room, that there's no tingling down your spine when I touch you? Do you think I don't realize that when we're apart, you don't yearn for me?

"Our holiday in England was the first time you were excited, almost thrilled to be with me. I dare say it was more about the surroundings and the others than about me. I'm the same man here and now as I was then, but the connection we had then is gone." He said it with acceptance and finality.

I couldn't deny or refute any of what he had said. He was right. I realized that I had been postponing the inevitable, hoping to have a change of heart. He was a good man, a great catch, someone who most women would fight for, and I was letting him slip through my fingers.

Trey paid the bill, then hailed a cab and took me back to my apartment. I wept silently the whole way, helpless in preventing the end from coming. He followed me inside and I flung my arms around his neck, burying my face in his shoulder, and sobbed as he held me close stroking my hair and whispering, "It's alright. Shhhh, everything will be alright."

The irony of the situation registered somewhere in the recesses of my mind. I'm refusing his proposal, yet he's consoling me. Life was indeed a mystery.

Gradually, I calmed and pulled away from him. Staring into the crystal blue of his eyes, I removed the engagement ring from my finger and held it out to him. "I envy the woman who will one day wear this ring," I said, managing a watery smile.

"Thank you," he replied with a slight nod of his head, and the beautiful symbol of eternal love disappeared into his pocket.

"Promise me that we'll remain friends. I couldn't bear life without you."

"My feelings precisely."

"Promise," I insisted.

In his most dignified voice he declared, "On my honor, I swear to always be your friend. I will remain a part of your life so long as you will have me." Then he took my hand and kissed it.

A wave of relief washed over me. I trusted Trey's word without exception. His promise was important to me and brought me even greater comfort than I expected.

Chapter Seventeen

I was a mess. It had been five days, maybe six (who was counting) since Trey had ended our engagement. I had holed up in the apartment, not wanting to see or talk to anyone except the delivery boys. Pizza boxes, hamburger wrappers, cartons of Chinese takeout, Krispy Kreme bags, and squashed Pepsi cans were strewn everywhere. From the kitchen to the bedroom, a trail of Doritos had been smashed underfoot. The bed sheets were full of crumbs and chocolate smears. A half-eaten carton of Ben and Jerry's Cherry Garcia ice cream dripped down the leg of the nightstand. When the cleaning lady showed up one day, I kicked her out as she shook her head and finger at me while reciting a litany of versions of shame-on-you, in Spanish. I kept the television on twenty-four hours and watched one soap opera after another, sympathetically crying along with those chronically ill-fated souls.

Between the food and the tears, I thought of Trey. He was right. Much as I would like to, I couldn't fault him for ending our engagement. I loved the idea of being married and I loved him, but I couldn't marry him, even though it would have been the perfect solution to my problem. I would never again have had to worry about being alone. I knew with absolute certainty that he would have cared for me and loved me every day of his life.

Sophisticated and well-heeled on the outside, on the inside I was still the simple midwestern girl from the suburbs who wanted more than anything to share her life with the man she loved. To come so close, yet still have happiness out of reach was torture. Life had played another of its jokes on me, but I wasn't laughing.

I was tired. Tired of trying to do the right thing. Tired of trying to figure things out. Tired of pushing myself to be better, do better, work harder. And all for what? I always ended up alone anyway. Might as well accept it, embrace it, and even revel in it. It was out of my control. Fate would determine my life, my future, regardless of what I did or didn't do. It was out of my hands. I needed to stop fighting it and go with the flow.

Clearly, my destiny was to be alone. The writing was on the wall. My parents had been taken from me when I was just a child. Angie, my greatest comfort and support, met an early death. The men I dared love always left for one reason or another. How much more proof did I need? I had to accept my fate, whatever it might be. With firm resolve, I vowed to accept the life that was given me from now on and not ask for more.

When I finally hit bottom and was done crashing, the damage was colossal. Mustering the courage to look in the mirror, I was horrified at the stranger staring back. My pajamas, unevenly buttoned and stained with a smorgasbord of junk food, protruded at the stomach with my new little addition, a carb paunch. I found a French fry among the knots in my greasy hair. My face and eyes were swollen from salt and tears, respectively. The apartment would suffer permanent stains on the carpeting and furniture. I had to offer the cleaning lady a bonus to get her to come back. My answering machine had recorded so many messages it had run out of space. I had turned the volume off and guilt crept over me as I listened to the voices of concerned friends and family asking why I hadn't returned their calls. People care, I told myself. I'm not alone.

I spent a couple of days recuperating and doing damage control. I started eating healthy, balanced meals, attended my aerobics classes, and ran in Central Park. I returned phone calls and email.

I returned to work Monday wearing black to disguise the paunch that remained. Prepared to field questions and comments about our breakup, I was relieved when there were none. Apparently Trey had said what was necessary to hold the staff at bay.

I had expected there to be awkwardness between us, but he was pleasant and talkative, sticking to safe topics. He was cautious not to avoid me, and during the staff meeting asked me to comment on several issues.

The week progressed uneventfully, but I was relieved when the weekend arrived. Putting on a happy face was exhausting, even though I had only aimed for a notch above devastated. Aside from my workouts, I looked forward to sleeping through Saturday and Sunday. During the week, Rick had called asking me to dinner, but I had begged off with the excuse that I wasn't feeling well. Which was true, in a way. The very thought of getting involved with anyone, let alone him, made me sick to my stomach. Another man meant another heartbreak and another binge and I didn't have the stamina for it.

The following week flew by. My concentration returned, and the week was immensely productive. I put the final touches on my manuscript, and was excited that it was ready for publication.

I was running along the path around the reservoir Friday afternoon when I could have sworn I heard my name. Uh oh, it has to be Rick, I thought. I tensed, but ignored the call, hoping that I was mistaken. I heard it again, this time louder, too loud to ignore. I looked back and saw Rick sprinting toward me. Damn, I have to find a new route, I thought, mentally adding that to my To Do List, but for now I was stuck. I slowed to a walk as he caught up to me.

"You're a difficult woman to catch," he said between gasps for air. He was smiling and his eyes twinkled with innuendo.

Despite my irritation, I felt a flutter in my chest, irritating me all the more. "Then perhaps you shouldn't try," I answered in my haughtiest tone.

Not to be thwarted, Rick's smile widened, "But I love a challenge, and even more, the sweet taste of victory." His devilishly dark eyes lowered to rest on my mouth.

The heat was instantaneous and rose up my neck to my cheeks. If only there were a cure for that, I wished, as he laughed heartily, obviously enjoying my reaction.

"I'm glad you're feeling better," he said.

"Yes, thank you, it must have been something I ate."

We ran in silence, observing the sights around us. I picked up the pace, hoping to end this contrived meeting as quickly as possible.

As we rounded the last curve, Rick said, "There's a new impressionist exhibit that just opened at the museum. How about if I come by at, say, five. We can check it out and then have dinner."

"Oh, Rick, I'm sorry–," I started.

"Don't be sorry," he cut in, "just say yes. I'll have you home early, I promise."

I could say I had plans, but he'd know that I was lying. Maybe it would do me good to get out. Our last dinner had been harmless and fun. "You promise?" I asked, weakening.

"Trust me," he whispered, making a face that indicated that that was the last thing I should do.

How had I let him talk me into this, again, I asked myself over and over as I showered and changed into my black suit, still camouflaging the remains of my eating expedition. I wore a gold knit jersey under the jacket and tied a black and gold scarf at my neck. Fussing to arrange the knot just right, I remembered that I had bought the scarf in Paris for Angie. I stopped cold. How I missed her. What would she think of me seeing Rick? Before I came up with an answer, the doorbell rang. I tugged at the scarf, trying to remove it, but the knot I had made was tight. I gave up and ran to answer the door.

"Sorry I'm late. Last minute business call from the West Coast." Rick, unlike Trey, generally ran late. "Ravishing, you look absolutely ravishing. The scarf suits you, Cherie." Also unlike Trey, he noticed and appreciated every detail. By the time he was done, you generally forgot that he had kept you waiting.

"Thanks, but no need to waste your charm on me." I tried to appear immune to his compliments.

He smiled and was a study in contrasts - the white teeth, raven hair, dark pupils against the whites of his eyes, his bronzed skin, the white open-collared shirt and black slacks, the black and white hounds-tooth sport coat. I leaned against the door for support, wishing I could unhinge it and take it with me. Extra support would definitely come in handy in fending off his charms tonight.

The exhibit was a magnificent sampling of the works of a variety of impressionist artists. Monet, Renoir, Cézanne, and Degas were all represented. Rick and I had seen some of the pieces previously at the Musee d'Or in Paris. They brought to life memories of the happiest moments we had shared. Monet's *Wild Poppies* was one of my favorites. When we got to it, Rick shoved his hands in his pockets and bent his head in thought. I gazed past the artist's strokes to the memory of us seeing the work for the first time and afterward making love in the afternoon. Neither of us said a word.

Viewing the paintings again was like reuniting with old friends after a long separation. It gave me a warm, uplifting feeling. Great art was food for the soul, something I needed desperately right now.

From the museum, we caught a cab to the Tavern on the Green. We sat beneath the crystal chandeliers sipping the champagne Rick had ordered. My thoughts were still with the paintings. "It amazes me how they captured the light, the essence of a scene, and suspended that moment in time."

"They are remarkable, but it takes someone with great sensitivity and inner beauty to appreciate them fully, as the artists would have wanted."

"Thank you, but I think the power of art is that its beauty brings out the sensitivity and inner beauty of the person beholding it. Feelings buried by the drudgery of everyday living surface in the presence of true beauty."

Rick reached across the table taking my hands in his. His voice was rich and low. "I couldn't agree more." He looked down at my hands as his fingers gently stroked them. Suddenly worried he'd see that Trey's ring was missing from my finger, I pulled my hands from his grasp, but it was too late. He had already noticed that the engagement ring was gone.

"What happened?" Rick asked, always quick to get to the bottom of things.

This was just what I had feared would happen, but I knew it had to come out sooner or later. I might as well get it over with. "It . . . didn't work out," I said, trying to cover the depth of my pain with a light, offhanded remark.

"Seriously, what happened?" His voice was sincere and his face clouded with concern.

I broke under his watchful eye. "It was me. It was all my fault," I cried, "I couldn't do it. Trey is a wonderful man. He was so patient, but even he has limits. I kept postponing setting a date for the wedding, so he ended it. He said it wasn't meant to be." I sniffed back the tears as Rick handed me his handkerchief. I dabbed at my eyes, blew my nose, and looked at Rick, waiting tentatively for his response.

He leaned in. "I'm sorry you were hurt. Trey sounds like a good man." He paused, then went on slowly, choosing his words carefully, "But I'm not sorry that it's over and that you're free. I'd be lying if I said otherwise."

Thankfully, at that moment, the waiter arrived with our entrees and delivered them with a flourish, breaking up the conversation. We gave our attention over to our dinners, and Rick entertained me with stories of his clients' recent foibles and the trials and tribulations of his travels.

After dinner we walked for a while. It was dusk and time was almost tangible as day transformed into night. Neither of us had much to say, our minds busily processing what had been said earlier.

Rick suggested we stop by a club that was a regular haunt of his and promised to take me home after a drink. I was relaxed now that the news of my broken engagement was out, and put up no argument.

The place was small, but classy, recently remodeled in an Art Deco style. The owner was a friend of Rick's and led us to a cozy booth where we wouldn't have to yell over the jazz band and their lead singer, a buxom black woman poured so tightly into a silver dress that the sequins looked like scales of a second skin. I ordered a Cosmo, this time because, as it turned out, I really liked the taste. Rick had his usual Cab Sav.

The band had been on a break, but now they picked up their instruments as the lead singer stepped up to the microphone. They played the intro and she began singing in a rich, bluesy style,

At last my love has come along . . .

My nerve ends tightened. My body, which had eased into a relaxed slouch in the booth, became rigid. Alarms were going off in my head. I've got to get out of here, I thought. "You know, it's getting late. I really should get going," I said, reaching for my purse.

Rick came around the table and slid in next to me. Not what I had in mind.

"You did agree to one drink."

He was going to hold me on a technicality. "Right. One drink." I picked up my pink Cosmo, which I'd only had a sip of, and downed it. "There. One drink. Time to go."

Rick shook his head and laughed. "Easy, easy. Okay. A deal's a deal." He motioned the waiter for the check. "They're playing our song. Is that what this sudden urge to leave is about?"

When in doubt, feign ignorance. "Song, what song? Oh, *that* song. Not at all. I barely heard it."

"It seems to have made you very uncomfortable."

Why wouldn't he drop it?

By now the songstress was crooning about finding the love you'd always dreamed of. The words oozed from her lips and poured over me like warmed molasses with the full heat of the impassioned torch song. She went on, moaning of the thrill of finally being so close to the one you love, feeling a thrill beyond anything you'd ever known. I felt my protective shell melting into a puddle, leaving me completely vulnerable.

The song was never going to end, the waiter was never going to bring the damn check, and Rick was never going to move out of my way. I'm doomed, I thought, as the edges of my mind grew fuzzy. I'm stuck here with him in this romantic little booth with no way out. It's fate, I sighed silently, and then I remembered the promise I had made to accept what came my way and not fight it. But not this. Surely not this. No exceptions, I warned myself. Making exceptions was cheating, I thought vaguely, as the champagne and Cosmo kicked in, blurring my mind.

The missing waiter finally appeared with the check. Rick reached for his wallet.

"No, I want to stay," I said, gripping his arm.

"Stay?"

"Yes, stay."

"Stay."

"I changed my mind."

"Changed your mind?"

"A girl has a right to change her mind."

"Definitely. I just wish I had a clue as to what's going on in that mind."

I smiled inwardly. It wasn't often I surprised Rick. It was worth staying to knock him off balance if nothing else.

"I'd like another, please," I said, holding up my empty glass. I was feeling bold now. I might as well embrace fate with open arms.

"Are you sure?"

"Why wouldn't I be?"

"You finished that last one pretty fast."

I tapped my fingers on the table and sighed loudly, "What's a girl have to do to get a drink around here?"

Rick was mystified by my new attitude, but he was not one to miss an opportunity. "This," he whispered as his arms encompassed me and he kissed me fully and deeply.

I kissed him back, savoring the taste of him. Cabernet Sauvignon had always been too robust for my liking, but it was perfect when blended with his lips. His kisses were exactly as I remembered, firm and flavorful and tingling. The only thing I knew at the moment was that I wanted his lips, his mouth, kissing, plying, probing mine more than I had ever wanted anything. If this was my fate, so be it. I would think about the fear and the doubt later.

When we stopped, we smiled into each other's eyes as the last verse of the song finished,

You smile, . . .
For you are mine at last

I never had my second drink. The cab driver snickered in the rear view mirror as he watched us kiss the whole way to my apartment. The elderly couple in the elevator smiled knowingly as we stood, wrapped in each other's arms, and the old woman's eyes twinkled when she wished us good luck while her husband helped her off at their floor.

Once inside the apartment, I clung to Rick and kissed him softly, sweetly, then teasingly, my tongue barely touching the edges of his lips, then with purpose and longing, leaving no doubt that I wanted more. He pushed me back and looked at me with hungry eyes, "Are you sure you want this?" he asked, his normally smooth voice husky with desire.

"I'm not sure of anything *except* this. I want you," I said honestly.

"Because I don't want you to regret it in the morning. I don't want you running from me afterward. Not tomorrow, or next week, not ever again."

"You don't know how hard I've fought to keep from running *to* you, Rick, how I've tried to deny what I feel for you."

Rick scooped me up in his arms and carried me to the bedroom, gently lowering me onto the bed. Piece by piece he undressed me, enjoying the unveiling with respect and admiration. His eyes shone like hot coals as he stripped and lay next to me, pulling me close and cradling me in his arms. He plied me with tender kisses and slow, deliberate caresses. There would be no rushing tonight. It had taken us years to reunite and Rick was determined to savor each taste and touch. With unhurried skill, he ignited my senses until a fire raged inside me from my head to my toes. His breath was on my neck and his voice in my ear, a primal beat reverberating through me. "I love you, Livie, I love you, I love you," he repeated, slowly unleashing my pent-up desire. The heat surged through my veins and I shook with a tension that was too much to bear. He brought me to the edge again and again as I groaned with pleasure. My entire being ached for him. He filled my body, my heart, my soul, building a hunger in me that only he could satisfy. When I was dizzy with the need for him, he came to me, and I clung fast, relentlessly seeking him. Then his mouth was on mine. "Together forever," he breathed into me.

"Forever," I moaned, with an honesty that came from the depths of my soul. "I'll love you forever," I cried, as our bodies jerked and surged in sublime triumph.

Minutes later, I lay with my head on Rick's chest, my body draped over him, still experiencing the tremors of aftershock rippling through me until gradually they subsided.

"You okay?" he asked, gently running his hands through my hair.

"I am now," I murmured, ". . . at last," and snuggled even closer.

Chapter Eighteen

Breaking the news to Trey would be difficult, but I wanted him to hear it from me first. Although others interpreted his aloof demeanor as unfeeling, I understood that our breakup had hurt him deeply. He had been nothing but cordial and kind to me since our split, but I noticed he used any excuse these days to have another person in the room with us at all times. I had no choice but to corner him in his office one evening after everyone had left.

I peeked in and knocked on the doorjamb of his office, catching him with his head buried in a manuscript. "May I come in?"

"Olivia, yes of course. What are you doing here so late?"

"I wanted to talk to you privately for a moment."

"Please, sit down," he said as he removed his reading glasses, leaned back, and waited.

Perched on the edge of the chair, I was as nervous as I had been for my first interview. "First, I'd like to thank you for making what could have been a very awkward situation as comfortable, or should I say as bearable, as you have." I was wringing my hands, wishing for a way to make what I had to tell him more bearable.

"I did nothing extraordinary. We are friends and that's what friends do for each other. I just happened to be in a position to help make things a little easier. But that is not what you came to tell me."

"No, it isn't." I swallowed hard and took a deep breath. "I don't know how to tell you except to just say it." I stopped for another gulp of air.

Before I could go on, Trey stated without fanfare, "You and Rick are together again."

Surprise and relief filled me. "Yes, we are. How did you know?"

"Olivia, something was holding you back throughout our relationship. You weren't conscious of it. Neither was I until recently. I've had time to think things through, and I realize that although you tried to put him in your past, and denied even to yourself that you still cared for him, your heart was never free of him, never free to love someone else. You were always waiting for Rick."

A stab of guilt pierced me. "I'm so sorry Trey. I never meant to hurt you. I hope you know that I would never do anything to purposely hurt you. Can you ever forgive me?"

"There is nothing to forgive. I know it was not done intentionally, and that I must accept responsibility for pushing things along more than I should have. Neither of us meant harm. We were just trying to find our way.

"I am glad you and Rick have found each other again. It's as it should be. I wish you the greatest happiness in your future together. You deserve it."

"Thank you. That means so much to me. You mean so much to me, Trey." My eyes welled and a tear escaped, running down my cheek. "Don't ever forget that," I said as he came around the desk to hug me.

"Don't ever let me forget it," he said, squeezing me tight.

It had taken us a while, but Rick and I had made it back to each other. It was remarkable really. We had both been through so much.

I had taken on a new career, one that had grown out of the anguish of our split. It had changed my life forever, totally and completely. Had it not been for our breakup, I may never have left the job I hated, to have my dream of becoming a writer come true. I had moved to New York and lived and worked on my own, building a life for myself. I had become successful and wealthy and, some might say, worldly. I had weathered a relationship and all of its hopes and disappointments. Trey and I had started out as strictly professional and had quickly grown into a warm friendship. Gradually, we had eased into a romance, only to revert back in the end and settle into a strong and lasting friendship. I had survived the loss of my beloved sister and from that suffering I had grown strong and confident and self-reliant, words that had never before described me. I still battled with my fears and insecurities as much as anyone, but now I knew what I was made of. I knew I could withstand the worst that could come my way. I still questioned whether I deserved or was worthy of the gifts that had been given me, but who is to judge which of us is worthy and which is not?

Rick, too, had experienced many changes. He had left his sales position and ventured out on his own, building a prosperous consulting firm that spanned the United States, Britain, and Europe. He owned homes and real estate across the country. He had a private jet waiting in a hangar and two pilots at his disposal twenty-four/seven. He had addressed his gambling addiction and had made a life-long commitment to keeping it under control. He had sown his oats, married, and divorced, and after all that, still had not found love.

To find us together again after such long and diverse journeys seemed nothing short of miraculous. It appeared to be our destiny. We could barely accept our good fortune. Frequently, in the midst of whatever we were doing, there would be a moment when one of us would pause and remark, "Can you believe we're together again?" The answer was always the same. We'd gaze at each other in renewed amazement and in unison chime "At last."

Rick and I spent every available minute together. Both of our schedules were busy and varied from week to week, making a routine impossible. We alternated staying at his place and mine, depending on which was more convenient at the time. I preferred my apartment because no matter how many cosmetics, notions, and lotions I hauled to his, I was always missing some necessity or other. And I knew he preferred being at his place because he could retire directly into his office to handle pressing business issues.

After Rachael had moved in with George, I had created a warm and cozy atmosphere, full of overstuffed sofas and chairs in hues of gold and peach and cream, and littered with pillows, knickknacks and flowers. Rick's apartment, however, was decorated following the minimalist dictates of Feng Shui. The clean, almost severe lines suited a bachelor's quarters or office, but didn't allow for the warmth of a woman's touch. I didn't like clutter, but I did like a homey atmosphere. We had not yet broached the subject of what to do about the situation.

My third novel was hot off the printing presses, and I was obligated to make a book tour that would last three weeks. At the beginning of my career, I had looked forward to the tours with anticipation as well as trepidation. I had shuddered at the thought of interviews and guest appearances, but looked forward to meeting my readers and signing their books, even though the tour schedule pushed my endurance to the limit.

I still enjoyed the interaction with my readers, but I dreaded the time away from Rick. He had decided to do some traveling of his own during my absence, touching base with clients he had not visited personally for some time, but he would not be gone long as he was nearing the end of his training for the New York City Marathon. It would be our first separation since we were reunited and I was in a panic. I didn't want anything to come between us ever again.

"I'll tell them I can't go, that I'm sick," I huffed as I packed and he lay on the bed watching me.

"No, you won't. You'll go and promote your latest novel and have a good time doing it. When you get back, I'll be here waiting for you. In the meantime, I'll call you every day. You'll be so tired of hearing my voice, you won't even miss me."

"Bet me," I said as I caved in to the urge and jumped on top of him.

Between faked moans and groans of pain from my landing, he wailed, "Sorry, I'm no longer a betting man." He saw the look of horror on my face when I realized what I had said. Gambling would never be a laughing matter for us.

"Oh Rick -"

"It's okay. No harm done."

I quickly changed the subject. "I should be back the day before the race." Rick had been training with unfailing determination. This was his first marathon, and I knew how important it was to him. "Maybe it's best that I'll be away. I won't be here to distract you."

"Ah, but you are now," he said, dumping me over and straddling me. He bent down and gave me an expertly executed kiss.

"I . . . have to pack," I murmured.

"Do you?" Again, his mouth sought mine with an intensity that was not to be dismissed.

"I . . . really should pack," I said, all conviction gone from my voice.

"Really?" he whispered, unbuttoning my blouse and kissing my neck as his hands tenderly caressed my breasts.

"Then again, there's always tomorrow," I sighed happily, forgetting everything and giving myself over to his touch, the taste and smell of him.

The next few days were filled with television appearances and interviews in the city and several book signings. Rick headed to the southern states to call on clients in Birmingham, Savanna, and Miami. When my commitments in New York were completed, I left for Cleveland, the first stop on the tour. I was welcomed as a hometown favorite, and enjoyed every minute of it. Wishing I had time to visit Laurel, I was scuttled off to Chicago, then on to Denver, Kansas City, Minneapolis, Seattle, and Los Angeles. Rick called faithfully every night, asking about the day's events and how I was holding up under the pressure. He always ended the call by telling me how much he loved and missed me. Just the sound of his velvety voice sent shivers of pleasure up and down my spine. In all honesty, he could probably have recited the alphabet and had the same effect.

Needless to say, I was ready and waiting at LAX for my flight to board on the first Saturday of November. The tour had been a whirlwind success. I was grateful, but exhausted, and above all, anxious to get back to Rick. When it was announced that all flights east were canceled due to a severe storm covering the entire eastern section of the country, I wanted to cry. After Rick called confirming that the East Coast was getting hit hard and advised me to stay put until the weather cleared, I was lucky enough to get a room at the airport hotel. At least

I would be close by to catch the first flight when air travel to the east resumed.

The storm that had paralyzed the city dissipated in the wee hours of Sunday morning. The dawn peeking over the horizon was clear, calm, and peaceful. The New York City Marathon, touted as the world's most celebrated road race, would go on.

To Rick, the Marathon was a metaphor for life, our journey with all of its trials, hardships, and pain. It symbolized the triumph of the human spirit, and affirmed the possibilities of extraordinary achievement. Thirty-five thousand athletes would embark on a twenty-six-mile trek through the world's most vibrant city. The course would cover the five Boroughs - Staten Island, Brooklyn, Queens, the Bronx, and Manhattan, five bridges, and finish up at the Tavern on the Green in Central Park.

The men's start time was ten o'clock. I caught a flight that landed at JFK at noon. As we approached the heart of the city, I bribed the cab driver to get me as close to the finish at Tavern on the Green as possible. Even so, I had to walk three city blocks to get there, actually running most of the way. I wasn't going to miss seeing Rick finish. The crowd of spectators was massive as I neared the finish line. I knew I would never get close enough to see him at this rate, so I pulled out my cell phone and called in a favor. The manager of the Tavern on the Green was a friend of Trey's. We had met several times and were merely what I'd call acquaintances, but Trey, at my suggestion, used the restaurant frequently for business lunches and dinners. After explaining my predicament and how very grateful I would be for any assistance he could provide, the manager pulled some strings and cleared a seat for me among the spectators.

I was barely seated when I saw Rick's unmistakable figure approaching. His face was pained, but his movements held to form from sheer willpower. Forgetting everything else, I jumped up, screaming and waving to him at the top of my lungs. The closer he came, the louder I yelled until he finally caught sight of me. He found the strength to wave and blow me a kiss. I stood beaming with pride as I watched him cross the finish line and accept the medal that was placed around his neck.

"That's my man," I exclaimed to the crowd in general in explanation for making a spectacle of myself. I left the spectators and worked my way to the family reunion area where the athletes, after being bundled in silver heat sheets and given food, met their families and tried to recoup. I found Rick in the crowd, seated and eating an apple and drinking Gatorade. I dropped to my knees in front of him. "You were amazing. I love you so much," I said as I wrapped my arms around him, never wanting to let go.

"You were pretty amazing yourself. I heard you over everyone else."

"I just did what I had to do."

"Will you do one more thing for me?"

"Anything. What do you need?"

"You, Livie. Will you marry me?"

My breath caught and my heart leapt. "I thought you'd never ask."

Hours later, after Rick had showered and rested, I cooked him a dinner of steak, baked potatoes, salad, broccoli with Hollandaise sauce, and Double Chocolate Cake.

Afterward, dispensing with television, the news, or any form of the outside world, we hopped into bed. I massaged and applied ointment to his still aching legs and snuggled close as we listened to some of our favorite tunes.

The Moody Blues had just begun "Nights in White Satin" when Rick shifted to face me. "Liv, I love you more deeply than I ever thought I could love another person. I'll try to show you the love I feel every day for the rest of my life. But in the meantime . . ." and from somewhere under the covers he pulled out the most beautiful ring I had ever seen, "let this ring be a symbol of my love and commitment," he said, sliding it on my finger.

I gasped, speechless from his words and the magnificence of the ring. It was a huge emerald-cut diamond with sparkling baguettes on either side.

"Did I do alright?" he asked fearfully. "Do you like it?"

Holding my hand out, I tilted my head this way and that as I scrutinized the ring. "I guess it'll do," I teased, but I couldn't go on with it. "Are you kidding? It's gorgeous. It's perfect. I can't believe it's mine."

"I can't believe that, after all we've been through, I can finally call you mine."

Chapter Nineteen

Now that we were to be married, we had to decide on a permanent residence. The apartment dilemma was solved when one of Rick's clients, Miles Leland, told him that he was selling his apartment on East Seventy-Second Street at Madison Avenue. Since Miles was spending less time in New York and more in his London home, he felt the large apartment was no longer warranted.

Rick and I loved it immediately. Spacious and bright, it had high ceilings and enormous windows. Cherry bookshelves and paneling adorned the walls of what would be Rick's office, and a small, but cheerful room next to it would serve as mine. Beautiful hardwood floors covered the living and dining rooms, while Italian marble spanned the foyer. The well-equipped kitchen was roomy and had a cozy nook for casual dinners. Best of all, Rick gave me free reign to decorate it as I wished, stipulating only that I not "girly it up" too much.

During the next few months, interior design became my passion. I consulted with a professional decorator, but I was determined that our home reflect our personalities and interests, so I enthusiastically took on the job of decorating the apartment myself. Paint charts, carpet samples, and material swatches were lugged from one end of Manhattan to the other in search of the perfect draperies to match just the right sofa and chairs that blended with the rich woods of the tables and consoles. I worked to incorporate our favorite old pieces, like the faded but still beautiful Aubusson rug, with the new.

Several months into it, the apartment was shaping up. Walls were painted. Carpets were laid. The furniture had just been delivered. On this particular day, I was on a quest for complementary accessories

– lamps, mirrors, pillows, and art – to pull the large pieces together and create just the right atmosphere when I stopped in a small art gallery in Greenwich Village. Something about it reminded me of the little gallery in Laurel where Rick had bought me the lovely pottery bowl I still cherished.

Caught up in my thoughts, I hardly noticed the woman standing beside me until she spoke. "Anything in particular I can help you find?" She had to be in her sixties, gaunt and bony of structure. She reminded me of a twig, dried and rigid, ready to snap. She looked as though she hadn't eaten a full meal in years, but her clothes were obviously couture.

"Oh, hello," I smiled. "I was just admiring your gallery."

"Looking for something specific?" she tried again.

"I'll know it when I see it," I said, as my eyes roamed the room and rested on a cobalt blue vase. I walked over to examine it closer.

"That is an exquisite piece. Venetian glass. You have a good eye."

"I just know what I like," I said, wishing another customer would come in and distract her from me, but instead, she stuck like glue while I inspected the vase.

I pictured it in our bedroom, with the ivory walls, blue comforter and drapes, and red Persian carpet. "I'll take it," I decided.

As she carefully wrapped the vase and rang up the sale, she became talkative. "If sales don't improve, we may not be here next year. My husband says there's no point in bankrolling an investment that continues to lose money. The gallery was my idea, to give me something to do since he works so much. I don't know what I'd do then," she said, her watery gray eyes lacking the emotion of her words.

"That *would* be a shame," I said, having trouble feeling sorry for her. "What does your husband do?"

"He's a banker at Liberty United Bank."

"Oh really?" I gained interest. "I may have met him at a charity event they sponsored last spring in Monte Carlo. What's his name?"

"Howard Laraby. And I'm Judith. Yes, he was there. And you are?"

"Olivia Townsend, with Horizon House Publishing. I don't recall meeting him, but then there were quite a few guests. He probably knows my fiancé, Rick Sloane. He also attended the gala."

"Rick, yes of course, we know Rick," she said with more enthusiasm than I thought her capable of. "The bank used his consulting services for quite some time. Howard said the Monte Carlo event was a real boost for the bank, enticing many international customers. And all thanks to Rick. It was his brainchild. But you already know that."

The words were barely sinking in. "Yes, of course," I smiled blankly.

"Too bad he's in such financial trouble, draining all of his accounts. I heard my husband talking about it with one of his colleagues at dinner the other night. Guess it's harder to take advice than give it. He's such a nice young man . . ." she drifted off.

I gave a preemptive glance at my watch. "I'm late," and grabbing my package from her, I headed for the door. "Nice meeting you," I said over my shoulder as I bolted from the little gallery.

People passed me left and right with their brisk New York gait, bumping and nudging me as I walked in a daze for blocks, trying to digest the information Judith Laraby had inadvertently given me. Rick had planned the whole Monte Carlo affair. It had been a setup to lure me back there and back to him. Was I flattered or furious that he had gone to such lengths to meet me? More importantly, was he in deep financial trouble? If so, why hadn't he told me? Come to think of it, I had made the last few mortgage payments, and had paid for most of the furnishings for the apartment. Whether he was rich or poor didn't matter. What mattered was our relationship. It had to be based on honesty and trust. How could I trust him if he wasn't being honest with me? And that led to the next question, his motives. Had he suddenly pursued me and renewed our relationship because of his financial problems? I was getting a bad case of déjà vu, remembering the pain his gambling had caused. Had it caused his financial ruin? Once again, I was totally confused.

My head was throbbing when I returned to the apartment and headed for the Advil. Rick wouldn't be home for several hours. I would take a nap and wake up clear headed. Then it would all make sense.

I awoke an hour later feeling refreshed, until I remembered the little gallery and what Judith Laraby had said, and wished it was all a bad dream. I dressed for dinner, wearing my cream chiffon Paris dress. Rick would be home soon and we were having dinner with Monsieur and Madame Gerard. For weeks, I had been looking forward to seeing Solange again and reliving all our wonderful memories of Paris. I decided not to let Judith Laraby's news dampen my spirits this evening. There would be plenty of time to get to the bottom of it. In the meantime, I would keep my eyes and ears open for any tidbits of information that might explain the situation.

Solange looked wonderfully chic in a black cocktail dress and long earrings, her hair pulled tight in her signature chignon. "It is good to see you again, Cherie. Success agrees with you," she said in her heavy French accent.

"Thank you." We hugged and kissed, cheek to cheek. "How are you? You look remarkable, as always," I said, admiring her innate sense of style. It was definitely a French thing. I found myself always feeling a little shabby next to her.

On the sixty-fifth floor of the General Electric Building, overlooking the Manhattan skyline, we ate in the Rainbow Room and toasted Paris while the band played "I've Got You Under My Skin." I had brought pictures of our trip, and we laughed and talked of our time together in France, never mentioning the disastrous ending.

Earlier, Rick had told them of our engagement and Emile ordered a bottle of Dom Perignon to celebrate. "To Olivia and Rick. May you share many happy years together." I smiled brightly, but doubt and suspicion crept into my mind like thieves, robbing me of the joy and anticipation I should have been feeling.

After dinner, Solange and I excused ourselves and made our way to the ladies' room. As we checked our hair and reapplied lipstick,

Solange questioned me. "Something is not right with you, Olivia. Do you not wish to marry Rick?"

The French were nothing if not direct. Her comment caught me completely off guard since I thought I had covered so well. I coughed and cleared my throat, choking on her words, but thinking that, as insightful as she was, maybe she could help. I took a chance. "How do you know when someone loves you, truly loves you, just for you?"

Solange's eyes widened in comprehension and she tilted her head up and cocked it slightly to the left in thought. After a moment she said, "You must know the person, really know him," putting great emphasis on the last part. Then she leaned toward me and whispered, "And you must know yourself." She patted my hand and said, "Everything will be alright. Now, let us not keep our delicious men waiting any longer."

When we returned, Rick invited Solange to the dance floor and I danced with Emile until we exchanged partners for the band's final song, "All the Way." As Rick guided me around the floor, he whispered in my ear, "I can't wait to be married to you. Let's set the date and make it soon."

Twelve hours earlier my pulse would have raced with excitement, but now my head ached from worry and doubt clouded my vision. I had to find out the truth, and soon.

Chapter Twenty

Solange's words weighed heavily on my mind. It seemed simple enough, "Know him and know yourself." I knew Rick better than anyone else. We had, after all, run the gamut of emotions over the course of our relationship. We had experienced the extremes, from floating-on-clouds happiness to heart-wrenching pain and everything in between. I knew him to be smart, sensitive, and sexy. He was caring, generous, and gentle. He was older and wiser than his years. He enjoyed a good steak and a good vintage of Cabernet Sauvignon. He loved classical music and ballet and, I believed, me.

I also knew his faults. He was a salesman, born with a silver tongue and slick as they came, but also as charming. He was chronically late, but always worth waiting for. He insisted on commandeering the remote control, but cuddled close throughout the programs. He could be arrogant and overbearing, but I admired his confidence and the way he took control of a situation. He was vain at times, but he worked hard and disciplined himself to maintain a good physique. He had a streak of temper, but it seldom appeared. When it did, it always died out as quickly as it had flared. He had an addiction to gambling, but had it under control. Or did he? I no longer knew for sure, but I had to find out.

The morning after our dinner with Solange and Emile, Rick was leaving for the West Coast, something he was doing quite frequently lately. In the last six weeks, he had made no less than four trips to Los Angeles. It hadn't bothered me that much since I was spending every spare minute decorating the apartment. This week I would use the time he was gone to investigate his financial situation, but before he left I had to confront him about the gala in Monte Carlo.

I poured the coffee, which Rick took strong and black, as we breakfasted on bacon and eggs at the table in the cozy little nook of the kitchen. "You know, just the other day I was thinking—"

"Uh oh, here it comes, what's on your mind?"

"I was thinking about the charity gala that Liberty United Bank sponsored. It was for breast cancer, a great cause, the one dearest to my heart in fact, as you know."

Rick continued eating.

"I wonder why it was held in Monte Carlo, of all places. I mean, why not London, Rome, or even right here in New York? Quite a coincidence, since that's where we had vacationed and had so many memories."

Rick was washing down his toast with big gulps of coffee.

"Horizon House had insisted that I be one of the writers to represent the company at the event. Trey said it had come down from the top execs. It still seems rather odd, don't you think?"

Rick set his mug of coffee down and finally looked me in the eye. "Okay, I'm busted," he confessed. "I set up the whole thing. Liberty United is a client of mine, and they needed to do something to improve public relations and increase their international business, so I figured I could kill two birds with one stone, so to speak. I pulled some strings to make sure you would be there. I thought it might be the only way for us to get past the problems I caused when we were there last." He gave me a sheepish grin, "Are you mad?"

"No. Actually, I'm flattered that you went to so much trouble to overcome any obstacles standing between us. The only part that bothers me is that you never came clean and told me you had arranged the whole thing."

"I always intended to, but the timing never seemed quite right. Sorry you had to find out from someone else. By the way, how *did* you find out?"

"You know writers never reveal their sources. That would be unethical," I replied smugly.

"Now who's keeping secrets?" he laughed, and checking his watch, said, "I'm late. The pilot will have a fit. I've gotta go."

I followed him to the door and we kissed goodbye.

"I'll call you tonight, Sweetheart," he said as he hustled down the hall.

Closing the door, I wondered at the irony of his comment about keeping secrets. Who's keeping secrets indeed?

I hated doing it, but I had to talk to Trey. After the Monday morning staff meeting, I followed him to his office. "Got a minute?"

"I've got all of ten, and then I'm off to another meeting. Please, sit down."

"I need your help."

"Certainly, what's the problem?"

"It's . . .well . . .personal."

He squared his shoulders and narrowed his eyes. "Perhaps I'm not the one you should be talking to, Livie."

"No, you are. You're the only one I know who *can* help me. Please, just listen," I pleaded.

"As you wish. Go on."

"You have friends at Liberty United, don't you?"

"Yes, but if this is about money, I can -"

"No, no, it's not that. I don't need money." I thought how sweet it was of him to offer financial help without even knowing the circumstances. Typical Trey. "What I need is information." This was even more embarrassing than I had expected. "I need to know Rick's . . . financial situation." I paused to gather nerve. "I have reason to believe he may be broke."

"And you fear he may be gambling again?"

I could only nod.

"Let me see what I can find out," he said, rounding his desk to me. He put his arm around my shoulders and squeezed me soothingly. "In the meantime, try not to worry. Stiff upper lip and all that," he said, smiling at his own British reference.

While I waited to hear from Trey, I thought long and hard about the "know yourself," part of Solange's advice. It wasn't as easy as it sounded. Some people spent their whole lives trying to "find" themselves, while others seemed to know from birth exactly who they were. I was somewhere in the middle.

I had learned a lot about myself since Angie died. I had become strong and independent, not aggressive, but tenacious. I had survived my darkest hour, and in doing so, had gained the fortitude to withstand whatever came my way. If I had to live my life alone, I would not be lonely. I had made peace with that. But I had to admit that I still faltered when it came to accepting happiness. I accepted my success as a writer because I worked hard for it, but when it came to allowing someone to love me, I had one foot out the door, ready to make a run for it before I became vulnerable. In way beyond vulnerable with Rick, the best I could hope for would be to cut my losses, make a clean break, and minimize the damage.

Suddenly, I realized that I had already assumed the worst. Rick's motive for marrying me wasn't love, but money. If I wasn't capable of trusting in his love for me and accepting that I was worthy of it, then we could not, and in fact, should not, go on. I couldn't live my life forever plagued with doubt.

The wisdom of old Madame Sophie from those idyllic days on the Mediterranean echoed in my mind. She had said that if love were nurtured, it would grow to someday nurture in return.

Finally, it came to me. I knew what I had to do. It was simple. It had been right in front of me all along. At four in the morning, I picked up the phone to call Trey.

"Hello?" he answered, groggy with sleep.

"Trey, call off your friends at the bank."

"Olivia, is that you? Are you alright?" He was wide-awake now.

"Yes, yes, I'm fine. Never better actually. Trey, listen to me. Cancel the search into Rick's finances."

"But you said -"

"I know, I know what I said, but I've changed my mind. I don't want to know. I don't need to know. Promise me you'll call and stop it. Please Trey, promise me."

"Are you sure you want to do that?"

"I've never been more sure of anything in my life. It's time I take a leap of faith and trust in Rick's love for me. I can't keep doubting and looking over my shoulder."

"But if he's gambling again, it doesn't mean he doesn't love you. It means he's got to seek help and get it under control."

"Exactly, and I'm going to be right there for moral support. I'm going to stand by him and love him no matter what. I'm not running this time."

"Alright, Olivia, if you're sure that's what you want, I'll take care of it."

"Thank you, Trey, thank you for everything."

"Rick's a lucky man."

I paused. "Yes, he is," I said, at last able to acknowledge my worth.

The March wind sliced through the air, sharp and icy cold against my face. My hair blew wildly out of control as I scrunched deeper into my coat. The runway and hangar for private planes was all but deserted. Rick's plane had landed and was taxiing into position. The sound of jet engines was deafening until the plane reached its assigned place. As the pilot killed the engines, the door opened and stairs unfolded to the ground. Rick, in leather jacket and jeans, descended the stairs carrying a bag and his briefcase. Halfway down the steps, he spotted me, and surprise, then pleasure, and then worry flooded his face. I ran to him as he strode toward me. "What's wrong? Has something happened?" he asked as he dropped the cases and held me at arm's length checking me over as if to find a wound of some sort.

Suddenly feeling ridiculous for being there, I stammered, "No, everything's fine. I probably shouldn't have come, but I . . .I just couldn't wait. I had to see you."

"Tell me what's going on, woman, before you drive me crazy with worry."

Another plane started its engines. "It's just that I love you and want to marry you, now, as soon as possible." The roar of the engines made it impossible to hear.

"You just what?" Rick yelled over the din.

Frustrated, I screamed at the top of my lungs, "I said that I . . ." The engines were cut and the roar ceased as I continued to scream " . . .love you and want to marry you as soon as possible." The last part carried with the wind across the open field. Several mechanics and stray passengers from neighboring planes clapped and gave Rick the thumbs up. He let out an exuberant shout for joy and grabbed me, lifting me off my feet, and we spun around and around as I clung to him for dear life. Because I finally knew without a doubt, that's what he was to me, my life.

Moonlight flooded the room and caused the sunset-colored walls to glow around us as we cuddled on the sofa listening to Mozart's Fifth and sipping champagne out of Waterford fluted glasses. We could have been drinking Pepsi out of paper cups for all I cared. I was in Rick's arms and nothing else mattered. I was quiet and calm; the serenity and bliss of the moment spoke for itself. Eventually, Rick's deep, rich voice resonated with warmth and love. "I have something to tell you, Liv."

I turned to look directly into his dark brown eyes, wanting him to see my unwavering support and reassurance when he told me of his financial losses and his relapse into gambling.

"As you know, I've been making many trips to the West Coast lately." He stopped and I braced myself for the worst - his confession that he'd gambled his fortune away in Vegas. "I haven't been completely honest with you about what I've been doing there."

Blurt it out, I thought tensely. I just wanted it out in the open. If he trusted me enough to tell me, I knew that together we could deal with anything.

"I'm in a tight situation right now financially."

Here it comes, I thought, and bolstered myself, ready to provide the love and support he would need.

"You see, I've sold off my West Coast clientele," he said, "so that I won't have to travel as much. I don't want to be away from you any more than I absolutely have to. Liv, what is it? I thought you'd be happy. I wanted to surprise you."

I had collapsed into his arms, overwhelmed with love and relief and joy.

Not understanding my reaction, he explained further, "I gave the buyers an extension on their payments. That's why I've been short on cash lately, but it's only temporary. It's a good deal, so I worked with them on the financing."

I realized that my whole life had been a preparation for this single moment. All the fear and doubt and loneliness had been necessary for me to reach this place. I lifted my head from his chest, smiled at Rick in the moonlight, and said the only thing left to say, "Can you believe we're together again?"

We held each other close, and my heart overflowed with joy... at last.

About the Author

A native of Northeastern Ohio, Mary Jane Smith began writing as an English major at the University of Dayton. Later, she pursued a career in accounting and became a Certified Public Accountant. She recently returned to her first love, writing. Readers the world over have enjoyed her work on www.wordshack.com. *At Last,* her first novel is being acclaimed by readers as a brilliant beginning for a new author.

Printed in the United States
74971LV00004B/1-24

9 781425 918460